THE BAD PARENTS

SL HARKER

Copyright © 2023 by SL Harker

All rights reserved.

No part of this book may be reproduced in any form or by any electronic or mechanical means, including information storage and retrieval systems, without written permission from the author, except for the use of brief quotations in a book review.

PROLOGUE

Detective Sandra Buchanan, a tall woman with a sharp-edged bob, steps out of her unmarked police car and takes in the street around her. Madison Lane. Not the kind of place she usually finds a body. Not among the flawless lawns and draping Wisteria blooms. Not where the houses are set back from the road with long drives curving to the street. The air is heavy with a velvety floral scent. Everything about this place screams privilege.

Two or three steps toward the crime scene, and that sweet floral perfume turns rotten. She's smelled it before. Blood. Even in the hazy early morning it's easy to spot the body. The deceased is bulky, probably a man, folded over on himself at the end of a driveway. She approaches slowly, noting the smear of blood running across the sidewalk. A tire mark brands the arm, which lies at a wrong angle, twisted and bloody.

Sandra stands, placing her hands on her hips, and looks at the road then at the driveway. *Why is there no blood in the middle of the street? Did the car come onto the sidewalk to run this man over?* Either the driver was completely out of control, possibly drunk or on drugs, or it was a deliberate hit-and-run. A murder.

The patrol units' arrival spurs her detective nature into action. She addresses the officers, directing them to set up a perimeter and search the area for anything that appears unusual. The officers fan out and tape off the scene. She watches them drop numbered cards near blood trails and the lone shoe in the house's driveway.

Sandra studies the shoe for a moment, turning it over carefully in gloved hands. Then she regards the house. One of her officers consoles a weeping woman standing in the doorway. *The wife or a neighbor?* Definitely the wife, judging by the tears.

If that's true, then this man barely made it out of his driveway before becoming roadkill. *How about that for luck?*

Sandra turns slowly, taking in the street. She feels eyes on her, sees a curtain close hastily over a window, notes the shadows of neighbors lurking behind blinds. And she wonders if here, on this quiet street, in this quiet neighborhood, in this quiet town, perhaps one of the neighbors had a not-so-neighborly reason to hate the man. If someone behind those curtains and blinds hated him enough to want him dead.

1

The door to the bar whooshes shut behind me, and I blink, adjusting my eyes to the dim interior. It's just after six, but already, patrons perch on wobbly barstools, nursing their beers. Let's face it, this is a dive. The floors somehow manage to be both sticky and gritty. Stale cigarette smoke lingers in the air. I gingerly pick my way across the room, scanning the booths with cracked plastic upholstery.

"Petra!"

I turn to see Dawn Lynes half standing and waving to me from a table near the back wall.

"We're over here."

Lifting my hand in greeting, I skirt a few empty tables and settle onto a rickety chair at the table.

"Good evening, ladies." I smile at Dawn and Amy. "So, this place is interesting." I wipe the sticky table with the edge of my hand. "Do they serve tetanus shots with your drinks?"

Amy Winstead, a petite brunette, titters nervously, her eyes flicking between me and Dawn. I don't know her well, but she's always been quiet and slightly nervous when I've talked to her at the neighborhood barbecues and block parties.

It doesn't help that her four kids are shrieking little whirlwinds and her husband, Miles, is useless with them. He's one of those "man's man" types. Too traditional to change a diaper. Brash and raucous, always giving the women smirking winks, like he's seen them naked. Amy probably finds it hard to be heard in her own house. Between us, Dawn and I have made it our personal challenge to bring her out of her shell.

"I know," Dawn says. "But it's the closest place. Plus, I can drink as much as I want without any judgment." She shrugs. "Anyhow, welcome to the first Madison Lane Moms' evening out. Anybody up for shots? I only have a couple of hours before I need to be back at the office for a meeting."

"Don't you work at the middle school?" Amy asks softly.

"Absolutely. Which is why I need alcohol." Dawn laughs. She shoves her chair back and struts toward the bar.

I glance at Amy. "She's kidding."

Her eyes widen. "Oh!"

"Amy, school shut hours ago, you know that." I laugh.

"Well, that's why I was confused," she says.

I pat her on the arm, hoping she'll loosen up soon. "Dawn's just a tease."

For a while, Amy sits very still. Only her fingers move as she picks at the edge of the table. She pulls them back and folds them into her lap when she notices me watching.

"How are you?" I ask. "Is everything okay?"

"Oh, um. Fine, I guess." Her smile is tight, her lips closed over her teeth. It's the same smile I give people I don't want to talk to in the grocery store. "How—how are you?" she finally asks.

"I'm fine, thank you."

This conversation is going nowhere fast, so I'm relieved when Dawn returns from the bar, balancing a tray on one hand.

"You look like a professional." I laugh.

Dawn gives a quick spin, showing off her waitressing skills before depositing the tray on the table.

"I waited tables all through college." She quickly passes out the drinks, glasses of water, and shot glasses full of a golden liquid. "Tequila!" Dawn announces triumphantly. "And vodka sodas," she adds just as Amy takes a sip and starts sputtering.

Amy giggles nervously. "Shoot. I thought it was water."

"Nope. Not tonight," Dawn says. "This is a special occasion, ladies. It's not often we get time with just us, no kids, no husbands."

I lift my glass to Dawn. "Abso-fucking-lutely. We deserve this. Between carpooling each other's kids, looking after our husbands, doing our own jobs, and living our own lives? How many fires have you put out this week, Amy?"

"Well, Aaron did stick a dime up his nose last Tuesday."

"And I bet you drove him to the emergency room," I prompt.

"Miles was in the middle of—"

I cut her off. "Miles knew you'd deal with it. But now it's time for you to unwind a little and let *him* put out some fires."

She smiles. "You're right."

Dawn grins at me when Amy raises her glass.

"To the Madison Lane Moms," Amy says.

We quickly pick up our glasses and clink them together. I'm surprised to see Amy take a long slurp of her vodka soda. Getting her out of the house seems to be working.

Dawn and I down our tequila shots, but Amy seems more hesitant this time. Dawn obliges by taking Amy's, too. And for the first time, I'm concerned. Dawn likes to party, but I've never seen her drink quite like this. Her glass thumps onto the table.

"Everything okay?" I ask. "You're going hard there, lady." I keep my tone light so as not to bring down the mood.

She waves a hand. "Yeah, great. Things are a bit hectic at work. I got passed over for that promotion I told you about."

"For the English department? What? Really?"

"They went with an outside hire." She raises her eyebrows. "And guess who's had to train him?" She scoffs.

"Jesus. I'm so sorry, Dawny." I grab her hand.

"Yeah, that's terrible," Amy adds. "Sorry to hear that." As Amy sips her drink, her phone pings, and she grabs it immediately. "I think I need to go."

"What? We've only had one drink!" Dawn sticks out her lower lip in protest.

"Miles is having trouble with the boys. I should go. He struggles on his own," she says.

"With his own kids?" I blurt. It sounded a lot more judgmental than I had intended.

Amy smiles thinly. "Sorry. There's dinner to make... and baths, I really do have to go. Thank you for inviting me, though. It's been so nice to see both of you." Amy stands, her hands brushing her skirt. "I'll see you for carpool." She hurries out, her eyes on her feet and her cheeks burning pink as she passes the bar.

"What was that about?" Dawn mumbles.

"She's a little shy, that's all. I mean, you've seen her at neighborhood functions. It's just the way she is." I shrug and sip my drink.

"No," she says. "It's more than that. Something's going on."

We're both quiet for a moment, thinking about Amy. We

know she has an overbearing husband. We just don't know if we have more to worry about.

Dawn breaks the silence. "It's a shame she didn't stay for another. I bet she has a wild streak just waiting for the right time to come out."

"Dawn, she's got four kids. I think we know when her wild streak comes out."

"True, true." Dawn cackles. "Anyhow, how've you been?" She settles back into her chair and swirls the ice in her drink.

"I've been, okay, I guess." The lie weighs on my tongue. *Can I tell Dawn I'm not really happy? That every day, I think that moving to the suburbs was the worst thing I've done? Do I tell her it's been almost a year since I've had sex with my husband? That my kids drive me insane? That I've lost so much of myself that I don't even recognize myself in the mirror anymore?* I'm not sure I can, but I can tell Dawn wants more. "The kids can be a bit much, at times."

"Hmm, yeah, I know what you mean. Especially when they're young. Even at six, Jamie takes up so much of my time. You'd think after the breastfeeding was done, they wouldn't be as 'hands-on,' I guess you'd say. Very clingy, you know. Always touching me," Dawn says.

"Oh my god, yes, the touching. I get so touched out by the end of the day. I didn't realize, before I had kids, how much of my body I'd literally have to give them." I shake my head with a sigh. "I don't know about you, but it makes it hard to get excited about climbing into bed with my husband at the end of the day. The last thing I want is someone else touching me." I grab my drink and gulp it, worried I've said too much. I feel Dawn's eyes on me.

"I know what you need," Dawn says. "Music. Come on. That jukebox has to have one good song." She points to the machine shoved into the corner, dust muting the neon lights.

She grabs my hand and pulls me up, laughing as she tugs me across the room.

"Oh, these songs are ancient." I laugh as I scan the list.

"Oh no," Dawn says with glee, "these are fabulous. Madonna? You know we have to."

Before I can stop her, Dawn shoves coins into the machine and pushes furiously at buttons. The machine hums and clicks, and the first thumping strains of "Material Girl" pour from the speakers. Dawn takes my hand and spins me around. Between the drinks and the swirling, I grow light-headed. And we dance right in front of the jukebox, the men stare at us over their pints at the bar. It feels good. Dawn spins me again, and the lights around me blur. Another song comes on, Spice Girls this time, and we bounce around, our hands in the air as we scream the lyrics.

Dawn heads to the bar and orders a few more shots, which we drink while dancing to nineties pop tunes. We must look like dorks dancing alone in a dive bar, but the alcohol buzz worms its way through my veins. Then the energetic beat slows down. I catch my breath and adjust my skirt, sensing those lonely men staring at us. The rhythm turns languorous. Whatever this ballad is, it has a sensual beat.

"I don't know this one." I turn to go back to the table.

"Oh no, we're dancing our way through all these songs." Dawn pulls me back to her and drapes her arms around my waist. She sways and takes me with her.

I'm feeling the drinks, so I just giggle and loop my arms around her neck, swaying against her.

Suddenly, I'm aware of Dawn in a way I wasn't before—her soft vanilla scent and the way her natural curls shiver around her heart-shaped face. Up close, her skin is almost perfect, just the slightest of puckers at the corners of her eyes from smiling. A freckle marks her upper lip, right in the center.

I lean forward and press my lips to hers.

Dawn stops moving and stiffens. But before I can pull away, her hands find my face, and her tongue pushes into my mouth. She tastes like tequila and lime. Her lips are almost desperate against mine, like she's searching for something in this kiss. I let her kiss me until my head buzzes and a chorus of cheers and catcalls interrupt us from the bar.

Dawn pulls back from me and studies my face. All she says is, "Well."

2

Dawn drops her arms and steps back with a laugh, but it sounds high and fake. "Tequila will do that, I guess."

"Oh, absolutely," I choke. "I don't know about you, but I've had way more to drink than usual."

"Especially since it's so early," Dawn agrees. "And hey, that was no big deal, you know." Her fingertips flutter over her lips before she drops her hand. "We let the drinks go to our heads."

"Absolutely," I say again.

"I think we ought to get an Uber home." Dawn pulls out her phone and taps at the screen. "You want to share?"

"What?" Her words snap me out of my thoughts.

"An Uber," she repeats. "I know I'm in no shape to drive. And I don't think you should either."

"Um, yeah." I'm still stunned by what happened, but Dawn seems to take it all in stride. I don't know. Maybe it's normal for her. Maybe she goes around kissing other people all the time. Even with the alcohol to blame it on, it still has me shook.

Mainly, because it just so happened to be the best kiss I've had in a long time. But I don't tell her that. Instead, I grab my purse and follow Dawn out onto the sidewalk to wait for our Uber. Neither of us say anything on the ride home.

All the lights are off in my house except a lone lamp emitting a yellow glow across the foyer. It's barely nine, but Andrew is an early riser, so he's probably already in bed. I shut the door and turn the lock, wincing at the shotgun-like crack it makes. Slipping off my shoes, I tiptoe across the hardwood floor in my bare feet and ease up the stairs, skipping the one in the middle that creaks.

In the moonlight peeking through the curtains, I can just make out the lump under the comforter that is Andrew. He shifts, and his light snoring stops when I push open the bathroom door. I freeze until the soft sounds of his snoring start again. I wait until I'm in the bathroom with the door closed before I flip on the lights.

Shucking off my skirt and blouse, I wrinkle my nose at the smell of liquor and stale cigarette smoke lingering on them. I shove them deep into the laundry hamper and make a mental note to drop off dry cleaning tomorrow. I debate a shower but decide it will probably wake Andrew. Instead, I splash water on my face. That's when I notice the smudges of light-coral lipstick around the edges of my lips. Not a color I would ever wear. I grab a washcloth, run it under the water, and scrub my face.

Did Dawn and I really kiss tonight? My slightly swollen lips and the feeling of guilt roiling through my stomach says yes. But like Dawn said, we let the drinks take over. *It isn't a big deal, is it? And really,* I tell myself as I change into one of Andrews' old college T-shirts and climb into bed, *it's no different than when I was at college.* Girls used to kiss each other all the time, mostly to try and excite the guys. This was essentially the same thing. We knew we had an audience, and we played up to it. Chalk it up to too much alcohol. That's all it takes really.

Andrew sighs and rolls over, his hand finding my waist. He squeezes sleepily, and the guilt rushes back. I turn my back to him, tuck my hands under my cheek, and try to sleep. For some reason, I can't stop thinking about Dawn's lips on mine. Then another intrusive thought pops into my head. *If the kiss didn't mean anything, why do I feel guilty?*

Andrew and I have always had a modern relationship. We've allowed ourselves space. He wouldn't care about me and Dawn playing up to a crowd by being a bit sexy, a bit racy. He wouldn't care about a kiss between me and a girlfriend as long as it didn't mean anything.

So I'm fine. *Aren't I?*

"Oh my god." I groan and pull a pillow over my eyes to shield them from the sun streaming through the crack in the curtains. My head throbs, and I groan again.

"You must have had some night." The bed sinks as Andrew sits on the end. "I didn't even hear you come in."

"You sleep hard. I sounded like a cow stomping around in the bathroom. Ow." I roll over and take the pillow with me.

Andrew laughs quietly and runs his hand over my blanket-covered backside. "How about I take the kids to the park for a bit? Give you some time to get over the headache."

"Would you?" Relief floods me when I realize I won't have to get up and make pancakes while the kids fight over the iPad. Then I remember what happened with Dawn last night, and the guilt rears its head again. "You don't have to." I swing my legs around and sit up, pushing the pillow away. My stomach lurches, and my vision blurs. I place both hands on my head and groan.

"I think maybe I should," Andrew says, his voice low. "You really want the kids to see you like this?"

"Okay, point taken," I say, noting his tone. "Just, don't take them to the place on Third. That playground always has cat poo in the sandpit. The park over on Maple is better, and it has bathrooms." I drop backward and pull the pillow over my head again. "Love you, babe."

"Mm-hmm. See you later. Love you."

The bedroom door snicks shut, and I'm alone. I close my eyes and drift to sleep again.

After a couple of hours of sleep, I force myself out of bed and into the bathroom. The nausea is gone, but the headache still throbs. I didn't even get home late, but those shots really did a number on me. Studying my swollen, bloodshot eyes in the mirror makes me wince. I turn away and start the shower.

Twenty minutes later, I feel better, if still a little shaky. Downstairs, I toss back a couple of Tylenol with a tall glass of water and look for the pack of saltine crackers that I know are in the back of the pantry somewhere. I settle in at the kitchen island with another glass of water and the crackers and watch the backyard through the window as I munch. The roof of Dawn's house is just visible across the back, three houses down.

I grab my phone and pull up her number, gnawing on my bottom lip.

Hey, should we talk about last night now that we're sober?

I put the phone down and finish my crackers and water. When my phone finally pings a text notification, I snatch it up. It's not Dawn though. It's Amy apologizing for leaving so early last night. I answer her with a *Don't worry about it, hon, it's fine.* Dawn still hasn't texted back, which makes me nervous. *Does she hate me now? How will she act the next time we see each other?*

I don't get the chance to worry about it anymore because Andrew and the kids come back from the park, announcing their hunger as soon as they pile through the door. Laughing, I pull the kids in for a hug before suggesting I make fried chicken tenders for lunch.

"Yours? Not the ones from the box?" Olivia's pretty brown eyes narrow with suspicion.

"Yep, mine. You can help if you'd like." I move to the cabinets and pull out bowls and ingredients.

"For lunch? Isn't that a lot?"

Andrew gives me an odd look, and I wonder if he can tell that guilt drives my reason for suggesting a home-cooked meal instead of sandwiches or something warmed up from the deli.

"Sure, why not? I've got the time." I lean up and kiss his cheek. "And you've had them all morning. Why don't you go catch a game or something? We'll call you when lunch is ready."

"I won't say no," Andrew warns me with a grin. "You're the best." He turns and heads back to the living room.

"Okay, monkeys, who wants to pour the flour?"

I pick up Luca and settle him on my hip while Olivia pulls a chair up to the counter.

"I do, I do," she chants.

So for the next hour, I patiently guide the kids in the art of frying chicken. And I don't think about Dawn once.

One of those statements is true.

3

"Come on, let's hurry." I jump out of the car and run around to open the back door and help Olivia unbuckle her booster seat. "I still have to walk your brother to pre-K."

"Cause he's a baby," Olivia says firmly.

"I'm not a baby," Luca retorts. The telltale signs of a tantrum flash across his face—the downturned mouth, the way his fists clench and his eyes narrow.

"No one thinks you're a baby." I fumble with the latches on his seat.

"Only the babies have their mommies walk them to class. Not like me," Olivia says proudly as she hitches her backpack over her shoulder.

Luca's face falls.

"Olivia, leave your brother alone. And wait for me before crossing the street!" I call as Olivia skips ahead to the sidewalk.

After getting the kids unloaded, I grasp them each firmly by the hand and pull them to the crosswalk, where we wait patiently for the crossing guard to guide us.

After sending Olivia down the hallway to her class, I lead Luca to his room, leaning briefly against the doorframe to watch him put his jacket and lunchbox in his assigned cubby. He turns and glares at me with a four-year-old's rage, so I blow him a kiss and head back out.

As I go over the day's errands in my head—stopping at the market, picking up a prescription, finding a gift for a birthday party the kids are attending over the weekend—I spot Dawn at the school gates. She never answered my text after our mom's night out, and I haven't run into her since.

"Dawn," I call, raising my arm.

When she notices and gives me a wave, I trot across the schoolyard to join her.

"Hi," I say breathlessly. "How are you?"

"Fine." Her eyes remain on the kids streaming in through the gate. "Good morning, Stacey. Colby, no running, you know better. Lovely hat, Sophia." She's in teacher mode, greeting both kids and parents. A moment later, her dark eyes flick toward me. "How are you?"

"Oh, fine, you know." I fidget, suddenly feeling a little ridiculous. "Um, you never texted me back."

"I didn't realize I needed to." Dawn continues to wave at the kids, greeting several more by name. "I'm busy right now, Petra."

"I—I'm sorry. I won't keep you long. I just wanted to know… um… did you tell Lewis? About Saturday night?" My voice drops low, though it's hard enough to hear over the din of the kids arriving.

Dawn's eyes regard me again. "Why would I tell Lewis? Did you tell Andrew?"

The line of kids dwindles, and a bell chimes in the building behind us.

"I didn't," I admit. "But I've been thinking about it.

Thinking maybe I should. I don't know." I stop and wait for Dawn to say something.

"I didn't tell Lewis because it wasn't a big deal. So we kissed." Dawn casts a glance over her shoulder before lowering her voice. "We were drunk, and it just happened. I'm not in the habit of telling my husband everything that happens to me. Are you?"

"No, I guess not." Her answer, along with her tone, rankles. Maybe she makes a habit of kissing people she's not married to, but I don't. Well, usually. "I just felt... I don't know... guilty is all."

At this, Dawn turns to face me. "Petra, don't be ridiculous." She laughs. "You have nothing to feel guilty about. It's not like we fucked. Didn't you ever kiss a girl in college? It's like that."

"Well, yeah, but that's not the same. I wasn't married then." I shift my feet, regretting that I came to talk to her. She doesn't seem to share the same concerns. I can't help but wonder if Dawn makes a habit of drunken kisses.

"Don't be such a prude," she says. "We got drunk. It's no big deal."

I chew on the inside of my cheek, searching for a way to tell Dawn I'm not a prude. I just don't feel right about not telling Andrew what happened. It's not like this happens every day.

Before I can think of anything to say, though, Amy spots us from across the schoolyard and heads over, her youngest, Hunter, strapped to her chest.

"Isn't he a bit old for that?" Dawn blurts before saying hello. From the way she looks at her feet, she regrets saying anything. Perhaps she's still riled up from our conversation.

"Hi!" Amy says. "Oh, um, maybe. He's three, but he's still small. It helps to have him strapped down while I'm corralling the other three." Her smile indicates she didn't take offense, but I still feel bad that Dawn snapped at her.

"Morning, Amy." I smile and notice the dark circles under her eyes. I'm not judging. I would be tired, too, if I had four kids. Sometimes it seems like I can barely function with two.

"It's been nice seeing you ladies, but I really need to get into the office. We have a few parent conferences to get through today." Dawn turns to go inside, but Amy stops her.

"Oh, just a minute. I wanted to check and see if we were still doing game night. At your house, right?" Amy turns to Dawn. "I don't know if you mentioned it on mom's night."

"No, I don't think I did." Dawn responds, her eyes sliding to me.

"Sorry I left so early. I just really needed to get home to the kids. But I look forward to game night." She shifts Hunter to get his knee out of her ribs. "Oof, Hunter, maybe you are getting too big for this. Anyway, should I bring something?"

"I wouldn't say no to a bottle of wine," Dawn says. "But it's not necessary."

"Okay, that sounds good! Petra, walk you to your car?" Amy gives Hunter a little bounce.

"Sounds good." I glance at Dawn.

"See you both at game night, then." Dawn turns quickly and heads away from us.

I hesitate, watching her leave. *What was that? Dawn seemed almost furious with me, but why?*

"Come on," I say, pulling myself out of my thoughts. "I'll help you get Hunter into your car." I run my hand quickly over Hunter's down-covered head.

We head down the sidewalk, and when I glance over my shoulder, I'm almost sure I spot Dawn standing at her office window, watching us go.

4

"Do we have to do this?" Andrew stands with one foot on the bottom step of Dawn and Lewis's front porch. "Honestly, I have work to get done at home. And wouldn't you rather watch some Housewives show?"

Grabbing his hand, I pull him up the steps. "Don't drop that wine," I warn, pointing to the bottle nestled in the crook of his elbow. "Sure, I could throw on sweats and watch TV, but we never go out anymore. Remember going out? We used to do shows, clubs, and concerts all the time before we moved here. Don't you miss it?"

"This isn't exactly a club, Petra," Andrew says. "Game night with the neighbors. I have to admit, not exactly what I thought we'd be doing when we moved." He reaches the second step. "But I hear what you're saying. I know I've been working late quite a bit recently. I'll try to make it home earlier sometimes. Maybe we can go for drinks or dinner soon. Just the two of us."

"Deal." I grin. "But we're here now, and I don't want to let Dawn down. So let's try to enjoy ourselves. Okay?"

He nods, and we cross the porch. As Andrew knocks

briskly on the door, my heart thumps. *What's wrong with me?* It's just a game night. I flex my hands, trying not to think about my last meeting with Dawn. She'd been so strange that day. So cold. Finally, the door opens, and Lewis, Dawn's husband, stands there smiling.

"Andrew!" he booms. "How's it hanging?" He claps Andrew on the shoulder and tugs him through the doorway. He turns to me, and his eyes drift from my feet to my head, stopping to take a healthy gaze at my breasts. "Petra, lovely to see you," he says, his eyes still on my chest. He steps back and waves me in. "Go on back. Dawn's in the kitchen."

I feel his eyes on my ass as we walk through the house.

I glance down at my cleavage. I guess I did put on a slightly tighter dress than usual. *But why did I do that for game night?* Like Andrew said, it's hardly the opera. Shaking away the feeling from Lewis's not-so-subtle gaze, I follow Andrew into the kitchen to find Amy and Miles already here.

They sit at the kitchen island with a tray of sliced meats and cheeses in front of them. Amy has a glass of wine in her hand, but she just seems to swirl it around. Miles, his tie already askew and his slightly thinning hair rumpled, quickly works his way through a bottle of beer.

"Hi, Amy. How are the kids?" I walk over and give Amy a quick hug.

"Oh, they're great." She puts down her glass and pushes it away. "They've got their favorite sitter tonight, so hopefully they'll be worn out and in bed when we get home." She laughs quickly like she's said something scandalous. "I mean, I'd love to see them before they go to sleep but—"

"Nobody cares about the kids, Amy," Miles interrupts. "I swear they're all you ever talk about. Let's try and stick to grown-up topics tonight, okay?"

Miles is a big man with a broad back and thick neck. Even

his fingers are thick. Amy is a sparrow to his hawk, tiny and delicate. I have a quick flash of the two of them in bed together, somehow figuring out how her petite figure fits with his hulking frame. I shake the thought out of my mind and turn to Dawn, who opens a bottle of wine and pours it into two glasses.

"Here." She slides the glass across the counter toward me before picking up the other for herself. "You need to catch up."

So that's the way it is. Things are still tense between us. Tomorrow, I'll call Dawn and set up a time so we can talk about what happened without anyone interfering. But in the meantime, I down my wine in a few quick gulps and push it back toward Dawn.

All she does is raise an eyebrow before pouring me another glass.

After a few minutes of small talk, Lewis claps his hands together and rubs them, looking around at the group. "Okay, who's ready to get their ass whooped?"

Andrew and Miles immediately boo him, and they all stand and head toward the family room, punching and ribbing each other. Dawn, without a word, gestures toward me and Amy, and we get up and follow the men.

We've hosted a few game nights, and somehow, it always ends up like this. I like to think of mine and Andrew's relationship as one of equality, or at least a tentative sixty-forty when it comes to housekeeping and child-rearing, but at every single one of these outings, "the boys" break off from us. We're soon pushed into typical male and female stereotypes, like it's inevitable every time we become a pack.

I pull at my tight dress as we enter the room. It's almost completely filled by a huge U-shaped sofa with a lacquered coffee table anchoring the center. A pile of game boxes occupies the table. I take in the rest of the room, noting the framed TV that I've been hinting would look great in our family room. Abstract paintings decorate the walls, and the floor is a light oak color. It's exactly the sort of room I imagined in Dawn's house, modern and cool.

"Okay." Lewis flops onto the sofa, his drinking threatening to spill. "What shall we play?"

"Lewis, be careful." Dawn slides a coaster toward him. "Have a seat." She gestures to the rest of us.

We all settle onto the sofa.

"I know we don't want Monopoly," Lewis says. "Takes too long. Pictionary? Cards Against Humanity?"

"How about some trivia?" Miles suggests.

I can tell he thinks trivia is his thing. I just nod and down my second glass of wine before reaching for the bottle Dawn brought from the kitchen. Andrew catches my eye and gives me a look. I just shrug and take a large sip.

Everyone agrees on trivia, and Lewis opens the box, taking out the cards and reading the instructions aloud to us. When he finishes, we decide to have our first game with our spouses as partners.

It doesn't take long before we're all teasing each other and laughing at some of the answers given. Except for Dawn. She put herself far from me and seldom even looks in my direction. The only time I catch her eye is when Lewis pours me another glass of wine. Her lips tighten, reminding me of how she tasted when we kissed. That touch of bitter tequila with the citrus lime kick. I know my cheeks flush red, but I hope if anyone notices, they'll think it's just the wine.

"Okay, okay. One more for this round." Lewis holds a card in front of him. He looks at Dawn. "Get this one right, and that's our second-round won." He clears his throat and reads, "Name the 1882 marble piece that was sculpted by Auguste

Rodin." He lowers the card and looks around, anticipation on his face.

"Oh, um." Miles snaps his fingers, searching his brain for the answer.

"Time's almost up," Lewis says, turning the timer around.

"*The Kiss*," Dawn says.

Lewis jumps up and points at Dawn. "Correct. *The Kiss*," he crows. "Second round to us."

It's so stupid, but the irony of the question hits me. The *kiss*. It's the elephant in the room, and someone just shouted it out. A bubble of laughter rises up from my throat, and before I know it, I'm tilting forward, one hand over my mouth, trying to hold it in. And it's not like a subtle titter or a chuckle that can be explained away. It's a hearty, chesty guffaw that won't end. Even with one hand over my mouth, it's loud, coming involuntarily from my body. Soon, tears roll down my cheeks, and I can't seem to stop.

"Honey, what's so funny?" Andrew's brow wrinkles. He reaches over and pulls my wine glass out of my hand.

"Nothing." I wipe away the tears.

Dawn stares at me, her expression so cold it could chill our drinks.

"Well, clearly, that's not true," Andrew says.

I can tell he's concerned. I don't erupt into fits of uncontrollable laughter every day.

"Just leave it," I say.

"We're all intrigued now," Miles adds.

My entire body is warm from wine. The room seems to tilt. Damn. I had more wine than I thought. "It's just ironic." I bite my lip. I hadn't meant to say that. Shit.

"Petra, hush." Dawn stands and crosses her arms over her chest. "I think we should call it a night. I've got a long day tomorrow." She bends to collect the game cards from the table, shoving them back into the box without straightening them.

"Oh, that's typical," I say. "You insist on getting us drunk then kick us out."

"Come on," Amy says quietly to her husband, tugging on his arm.

"No way." Miles grins. "Something's going on here."

"Yeah. Someone want to tell me what?" Lewis looks between Dawn and me, his brow wrinkling.

"It's nothing. Just a little... disagreement." Dawn slides the lid back onto the box and places it on the stack before straightening and facing Lewis. "You know, we just had a bit much to drink on our mom's night out."

"Disagreement? Like hell. You kissed me," I blurt.

The room goes quiet, and every eye is suddenly on me. Dawn closes her eyes and shakes her head.

Andrew puts a hand on my shoulder and turns me. "Petra?" he says, his voice questioning.

"Sorry," I say, "it's true though. We kissed at the bar. But it didn't mean anything."

I grab his arms as he crosses them over his chest. He doesn't say anything to me.

My heart hammers against my ribs. *What have I done? Why couldn't I just keep it to myself?* My eyes lock on Andrew's. His expression is unreadable. The room is silent.

5

Lewis belly laughs. "Is that why you two are acting weird? Baby, if you're stressing, there's no need. Seriously, I think it's kinda hot. Hey, you ladies want to do it again? Give us a little show?" Lewis looks between me and Dawn and wriggles his brows suggestively.

"Did you really kiss?" Amy's quiet voice breaks through Lewis's laughter.

"Yes, we did," Dawn finally says.

She watches me with a thunderous face, and it makes me want to shrink away. I think briefly that I should give up drinking. It appears I can't have a few drinks without making a complete ass of myself.

"Oh, man, sounds like you missed out, babe," Miles says to Amy. "Maybe you should have stayed. The three of you—woo." He pulls at his shirt collar, grinning the entire time.

A flush travels over Amy's face, coloring her scarlet. She studies her feet.

Andrew doesn't say a word. He just sits on the sofa, his arms crossed, brows pulled low. His lips tighten.

"It was nothing," Dawn says. "We'd had some tequila

shots, and some guys were watching us dance at the bar. We just thought we'd put on a show, that's all."

"Sorry, I don't understand," Amy says. "Didn't you cheat on your husbands? I don't know why no one is freaking out. It seems like a very big deal to me."

"Look, my wife is straight," Lewis says. "So it isn't cheating. At least, not as far as I'm concerned."

Miles shrugs. "Are those the rules?"

"I mean, it makes sense to me." Lewis grins. "Hey, babe, it's not a big deal. I'm not mad or anything. I'd just like to be included next time!"

Lewis and Miles dissolve into fits of adolescent snickering. Andrew remains silent.

"Honey." I perch carefully next to him. "It was just... it didn't mean anything. You know that, right? I'd just had too much to drink. It won't happen again."

A door slams somewhere deep inside the house, and I look around to see Dawn has disappeared. "I'll be right back," I say to Andrew.

He mumbles something inaudible. I squeeze his knee before making my way back into the kitchen. Then I see Dawn through the window, standing on the edge of the patio, and follow her out.

"Dawn?" My heels click as I cross the concrete pavers. "Are you okay?"

She turns her head, and I'm stunned at the venom in her eyes. "No. I'm not. I thought it was clear that the kiss was just between us. But then you go and tell... everybody. Just blurt it out in front of a roomful of people."

"Sorry." I step closer and reach for her arm. "I really am. I know I've had too much wine. But really, I didn't think it was a big deal. Right? That's what you keep saying. It didn't mean anything. It's no big deal."

"It's not... it didn't. But still..." She trails off and looks away again.

"Then why does it matter if I told everyone? Lewis doesn't seem to care." I swallow the lump building in my throat.

"Andrew didn't look happy."

"You're right. And that's something he and I will have to deal with. But it's out now. And frankly, I'm relieved. I wanted to tell Andrew from the beginning. I didn't feel right about keeping it a secret, especially since you didn't think it was a big deal."

"Oh, so because you felt guilty, you thought it would be a good idea to just blurt it out in front of everyone. I work at a school, Petra. If something like this got around..." She stops, her jaw grinding. "You shouldn't have done that."

"I'm sorry. I really am." I throw up my hands. "Let's just put it behind us. I'll deal with Andrew at home. And I'll talk to Amy, too. Okay?" I put my hand on Dawn's shoulder, pleased when her stiff back loosens beneath my touch.

"Fine. Talk to them both. Then, let's put this behind us." Dawn picks up my hand, pats it gently, and lets it fall before turning and walking back into the house.

I wait for a moment, allowing her to go ahead of me. Through the window, I watch her pour a fresh glass of wine then leave the kitchen, heading toward the den. With a sour feeling in my stomach, I follow her in.

Everyone is on the sofa when I enter. I settle down beside Andrew, who still hasn't said a word to me.

"Now that we've had our drama, what shall we do?" Miles asks.

"I think maybe we should go home," Amy says softly. "I'm sure everyone else has enough to talk about without us around."

"No, no, no. It's early still," Lewis interjects. "There's no reason to go. You're good, right?" He looks between me and Dawn. "Everybody's a grown-up here, right?"

"Andrew?" I ask. His silence worries me. The only other time I've seen him this quiet was when his brother borrowed his car and brought it back with a huge dent. "Are we okay?"

He just shrugs.

"So, what should we do?" Miles grins.

"I know what we can do." Lewis smirks. "Let's play spin the bottle."

6

"Absolutely not," I say. "Have you lost your mind?"

Amy lifts a palm. "I don't think that's a very good idea. With everything that's already gone on? It's... we have vows."

Standing, I grab Andrew's hand and pull him to his feet. "I think we'd better just go home."

Andrew pulls his hand away from mine. "No, we're staying. I want to play." His voice is low and cold, and he avoids my eyes. "We're staying." He drops back onto the sofa.

I immediately stiffen, stung by his tone. But I don't want to push it, considering my confession tonight. So I sit back down, hoping he'll snap out of whatever he's going through.

"Well, I think we should do it," Dawn says. "It's not cheating if we all consent. It's just a bit of fun between friends."

I almost roll my eyes. It's like she's trying to prove something to herself. Then I wonder why. *What's going on with her?*

In the end, I just shake my head. "Fine. We're all adults." Then I glance at Amy. "If you're not comfortable with this, you can say no."

She directs her gaze toward her husband. Her eyebrows raise toward her hairline, and I see her concern. But Miles grins like he can't wait.

"Amy's up for it. Aren't you?" He strokes her hair like she's a dog, and heat flares in my cheeks. I can't stand the way he treats her.

She nods. "Sure. It'll be fun."

Lewis disappears into the kitchen and comes back with an empty wine bottle while Dawn and Miles move the coffee table out of the way. We all settle onto the floor in a sloppy circle, and Lewis puts the bottle at the center, giving it an experimental spin.

"Okay, a few rules," he says.

"Is that really necessary?" Dawn huffs exasperatedly.

"All games have rules," Lewis replies.

She shrugs. "What are the rules?"

Lewis raises a finger. "All right then, rule number one, the bottle has to complete one full rotation. Number two, you can't pass your turn. And number three, you have to kiss whoever the bottle lands on, boy or girl, doesn't matter."

"I'm not sure about the third rule." Miles gives Lewis a sideways glance.

"Take it or leave it," Lewis says.

"All right, fine," Miles conceded. "Shouldn't we rock, paper, scissors to pick who goes first? That's how we did it in high school."

"No, it's my house and my wine bottle. I'm spinning first. Watch out, ladies." Lewis winks. "Okay, here we go." He leans forward and gives the bottle a spin.

We all watch, holding our breath. The bottle spins quickly at first before finally starting to slow, and I watch with dread as it slows, slows, then stops, the top pointing right at me.

I glance guiltily at Andrew. *Is this really what he wants? To see me kiss one of his friends?* The thought makes my blood run cold, especially considering the way Lewis looked at me when I walked in tonight.

"Is this okay?" I mumble.

"You heard the rules," Andrew replies.

"All right." Glee colors Lewis's voice. "Looks like it's you and me, Petra." He beckons me with one finger and a sneer.

I try to compose my face and keep from rolling my eyes as I stand and cross the floor to where he sits. Bending over, I purse my lips and aim for his cheek. It's not enough.

Lewis turns his head, and my lips land squarely on his. Before I can step away, Lewis grabs my face and presses his tongue into my mouth. His lips feel chapped and taste like he had something with onions for dinner. It's harsh, and I can't help but think about how soft and pliable Dawn's lips had been, how even though our kiss had an edge of desperation to it, it was still silky, still sensual. This was nothing like that. Lewis's teeth clash against mine, and his tongue feels like sandpaper as it roams through my mouth. I still allow it, though I barely kiss back.

When it's over, Lewis whoops. "That's how it's done."

I rub the back of my hand over my stinging lips and slink back to my seat. When I look up, Dawn glares at me, her eyes sparking with anger or jealousy or both. I'm not sure. Andrew won't even look at me. His head is turned as he studies Lewis. And when I grab for his hand, he pulls away. My sinking stomach tells me that this was a very bad idea. But I can't take it back, and I don't know how to stop it.

"Okay, Dawn, your spin," Lewis announces.

He sits back and watches as his wife spins the bottle. When it lands on Andrew, my chest tightens.

Dawn glances at me, then my husband. Something hard flashes across her face before she moves across the floor and drapes herself on Andrew's lap. Andrew cradles the back of her head and doesn't have to force her mouth open like Lewis had with me. The tip of Andrew's tongue darts out to taste Dawn's bottom lip. Then they both open their mouths as they French kiss.

"That's what I'm talking about," Miles hoots, clapping his hands. "That is hot. Get it, Andrew!"

It's a long kiss. *Longer than my kiss with Lewis? Longer than my kiss with Dawn? It's just a kiss,* I remind myself. We're friends having fun. But heat builds in the bridge of my nose and behind my eyes. I glance over and see Amy looking at me, and I can't stand the pity on her face. I turn my head away, staring into the corner of the room until Dawn and Andrew finish their kiss. When she sits back down, I refuse to meet Andrew's eyes.

The game continues until eventually everyone has kissed everyone else at least once. It doesn't get any easier, watching Andrew's fingers glide through another woman's hair or seeing Dawn press her lips chastely against Amy's. Or the embarrassed pecks the men plant on each other. But I keep going. And my last spin lands on Andrew. I lean over, thinking he'll just peck my lips, but he pulls me in close, draping my legs across his lap. His kiss is tender, but it holds an edge that burns through me, exciting me.

When we finish the game, Andrew helps me to my feet, his hand hovering over my lower back as he guides me to the door. And when I look over my shoulder as we leave, Dawn watches us, a small smile playing across her mouth like she knows a secret.

7

Andrew doesn't say a word on the way home, but his hand remains on my lower back for the short walk. He holds himself erect, his back like a ramrod with tension running through every muscle. He hasn't seemed so handsome to me for a long time. I can't stop staring at his square jaw and the side view of his long eyelashes.

Once we're home, Andrew pulls out a wad of bills without counting them and hands them to the babysitter, all but pushing her out the door.

"Bye, Kaitlyn, thanks," I call after her, but Andrew already closed the door and is back across the foyer, pushing my coat.

"Get this off," he almost growls.

I shove the coat down my arms and drop it on the stair rail.

He grabs my hand, pulling me up the stairs. Anticipation curls in my stomach, and I hurry down the hall with him, flinging the bedroom door open. We tangle together and fall onto the bed, our kisses rough and burning.

"What was it like, kissing Dawn?" he asks as he pulls off my skirt, his fingers skimming over my thighs. His voice is coarse, his movements almost frantic as he tugs at the rest of my clothes.

"It was good," I pant, tugging at his tie. "Her lips are the softest I've ever kissed."

"Hmm" is his only answer as he helps me with his belt and shoves his pants down.

"What about you? Did you like kissing Dawn?" I ask, surprising myself. I'm even more surprised to find that I hope he did. I hope she tasted good to him, that her tongue was soft against his and that he felt it all over his body.

Andrew pulls back and looks at me, his eyes knowing, a small grin playing over his lips. "She was wonderful. I wanted that kiss to go on all night." Then he pushes my knees apart.

"Will you be thinking about her when you fuck me?" I ask.

He thrusts into me, one hand wrapping around my throat.

"Yes," he says.

"What if I kiss another woman?" I ask.

He moans and thrusts harder. "Then I'll just have to fuck you even harder."

A thrill of pleasure works its way through my body. Andrew squeezes my neck, just enough that it feels good and doesn't hurt. Just enough to let me know he's in control. Then he pulls back, grabs my waist, and spins me over so that I'm on my knees. He seizes hold of my hair, yanking my head back.

"Are you thinking about her?" I ask.

"Yes." He grunts.

Then I come.

When I roll over and check the clock, Andrew is already up. The bathroom door is shut, but the light leaks around the edges and I hear water running. I stretch and notice that I never bothered to get dressed after Andrew and I finished last night. I'd fallen asleep with my leg tossed over his, my hand draped across his waist. That hadn't happened in so long, I couldn't even remember the last time. I roll over into his spot and find that it's still slightly warm.

But when I think of last night, guilt churns in my stomach. *Did we really kiss all our friends then come home and have the best sex we've had in ages? What kind of people does that make us? What kind of person, what kind of mother, does what I did last night? What do Dawn and Amy think about me? How can I face either of them? Or my husband for that matter.*

When the water stops, I roll over and bury my face in my pillow, pretending to still be asleep and putting off what I know will probably be a fight. I feel Andrew sit on the edge of the bed to put on his shoes.

"I know you're awake," he says quietly.

"Oh." I roll over and sit up. "I just—didn't want to, um." I stop talking because I don't know what to say.

"You don't have to say anything." He runs his hand over my disheveled hair. "I need to run to the office. Any plans for the day?"

"The office? On Saturday?" I shove the blankets off my legs and stand up, stretching.

Andrew's eyes follow the contours of my body. It appears we won't be talking about last night.

I hold my breath. This isn't like Andrew. He's a therapist, so we usually deal with everything by talking things out. In fact, sometimes we do too much talking. I kind of like this. Andrew hasn't paid this much attention to me in months. The game last night shifted something in our relationship.

"Just a few patient notes I need to take care of. I'd rather get them done today." He brushes a speck of lint on his shirt.

"The kids have a birthday party, but I'd rather spend the day with you," I say almost shyly.

Andrew's response is to cross the room and give me a lingering kiss.

"This evening," he says. Then he smacks my thigh lightly before leaving the room.

Two hours later and I'm in a swarm of sugared-up kids yelling like banshees. The party, like a lot of suburban events, is beyond ridiculous for a six-year-old. A petting zoo, balloon clowns, and a cotton candy stand all fit in the confines of someone's backyard. Add thirty kids and a bunch of aggravated parents, and it makes me want a martini and a dose of Advil.

I park Olivia and Luca in front of a magician pulling handkerchiefs out of a hat, warn Olivia to keep an eye on her brother, grab a lukewarm cup of punch, and sit down at one of the patio tables set at the rear. I grimace after I take a sip of the drink and push it aside. As I fan myself with a napkin printed with a colorful "6," a shadow falls over me. I look up to see Amy, a toddler resting against her hip.

"Hey." I shade the sun with my hand.

"Hi," she says softly. "Um, can I sit down?"

"Yeah, yeah, absolutely." I push out a chair with my foot.

We're both a little awkward, even more than usual, but after last night, I'm surprised Amy plucked up the courage to approach me. She settles into the chair, Hunter on her lap, and pulls a sippy cup and bag of snacks out of a diaper bag. After she arranges them in front of the toddler, who attacks the cereal O's with gusto, she turns to me.

"So, how are you?" she asks.

I can't tell if it's sympathy in her voice. *Does she feel sorry for me?* We were both at the same party last night. I don't need her pity.

"I'm fine. How about you? How are you doing?" I lean my arms on the table and look at her, arranging my face into what I hope is commiseration.

"Fine." I see her bite the inside of her cheek. She shifts Hunter around and hands him the sippy cup. "I'm glad I ran into you. I kind of wanted to talk."

"Oh, about what?" I grab my discarded punch and take a sip, just barely keeping myself from grimacing at the warm, sugary mix.

"About, you know, last night." Her voice drops to a whisper, and she looks around quickly to make sure no one else is within earshot. "Was it crazy? What we did? I'm not sure how I'm supposed to feel."

I take a deep breath and think about her words. "I think this is something you need to discuss with your husband."

"I'm not sure I want to. He seemed to be enjoying himself way too much," Amy replies.

I think I see the beginning of tears in her eyes.

"Am I a bad person for feeling jealous? I mean, I kissed someone else, too," she says.

I flash back to Amy kissing my husband, their kiss tender, not chaste, but not particularly sensual either. I'm not sure what I feel about it. A little jealous, perhaps.

"No," I say. "Not at all. It was hard for all of us, I think. I'm not sure why we did it. What about Miles? Did he get jealous of you kissing other men?"

Amy just shrugs. "Not really. I just... I can't stop thinking... Do you think that we all, I don't know, broke our wedding vows?"

"I don't think it was that big a deal. We're all adults,

right? Everyone consented." I'm not entirely sure I believe my own words, but I won't let Amy know that.

"I guess."

It's obvious I didn't tell her what she wants to hear. She doesn't say anything else, just sits feeding Hunter tiny pieces of snacks, her brow pulled down, wrinkling her pretty face.

"You can talk to me, you know," I say eventually. "If anything's on your mind or going on at home."

"What do you mean?" Her words come out faster, sharper, more defensive than usual.

"Nothing. I didn't mean anything by it."

"Okay," she says. Then she adds, "Everything's fine. I'm just worried about judgment. You know... from God."

"Oh," I say. "I understand. Well, personally, I don't think He cares too much about what adults want to do for fun. But maybe I'm just a bad person."

She shakes her head. "I don't think that."

I smile. "Good. Thank you."

She grabs my hand. "Maybe you're right."

I squeeze her hand. "I think God wants you to be happy. So do more of whatever makes you feel that way. Okay?"

Olivia takes a tumble over by the candy floss stand, and I go to kiss the boo-boo on her knee. After applying a Band-Aid, I decide it's probably time for us to go, so I collect my sticky kids and pack them into the car.

"Did you have a good time?" I ask, pulling out of the drive.

"Nathan puked in the bouncy house," Olivia says.

"Oh no," I reply.

I'm not sure how I managed to miss that drama, but I'm glad I did. Perhaps I was still talking to Amy at that point.

On the ride home, I answer my chattering kids with the occasional "mmm" and "oh yeah," not really listening to the stories they tell. Instead, I drive and consider my conversation with Amy. *Do I believe that we were just having fun? Or is Amy right in thinking that we all broke our wedding vows?* By the time we get home, I don't have an answer. In fact, I feel more conflicted than ever.

So, what am I? A whore? Or a fun wife?

8

It's been a few days since the birthday party. I haven't talked to Dawn or Amy. Our WhatsApp carpool group has remained completely silent, and I have to wonder if they're purposely ignoring each other, as well as me. Finally, this morning as I clean up the kitchen from breakfast chaos—I have no idea how Luca manages to get cereal on the underside of his chair—I grab my phone and think about the best way to initiate a conversation about something besides carpool or school activities. I settle on asking Dawn and Amy if they'd like to get coffee.

As soon as the message is sent, my heart patters. To pass the time waiting for a response, I carry on cleaning the kitchen, scrubbing the stove to give my hands something to do.

Amy replies first with a quick "sure," but I have to wait awhile for Dawn's answer. When she finally messages, it's to say it'll only work for her on her lunch break.

No problem, I send. *Is tomorrow okay?*

I can do one, Dawn texts. *At the café near the school.*

Relief floods through me. At least they want to meet.

Maybe we can sort this all out and clear the air. I think back to the first time I met Dawn. I was dropping Olivia off at school. It was her first day. Dawn had just started as a teacher there, and she patted me on the shoulder as a screaming Olivia went to her first class.

"The first day is always the hardest. I have one the same age. I guess it's a little easier when you work at the school where your kid goes." She saw me sniffing back my tears and smiled. "What's your daughter's name?"

"Olivia," I said.

"I'll look out for her today. Okay? Now go and eat something because I bet you skipped breakfast this morning, didn't you?"

I nodded.

Dawn has always been supportive, and she's always looked out for Olivia at school. I would hate to lose that friendship.

Marco's, the Italian café down the road from the school, is always popular, and it takes me a few minutes to locate a table. I finally find one toward the back and settle in after ordering my cappuccino. The place has a pleasant bustle to it. Coffee and buttery pastries scent the air. The sound of steaming milk hisses through the small space, along with the tail ends of people's conversations. I see Dawn when she walks in, her dark curls plaited and her blouse buttoned to the neck. She looks every inch the professional. She spots me and holds up a finger while she gets in line to grab a drink.

Amy finally appears in the doorway, pushing a stroller with one hand as she tries to hold the door with her other. I run over and maneuver the stroller out of the way so she can get inside. She thanks me and takes the stroller back, pushing it through the crowded café with a chorus of "excuse mes." After arranging Hunter with a sippy cup and toy giraffe, she sits down with a sigh. Her face is flushed, and her T-shirt looks like it's skipped a couple of washes.

"Hi," she manages to say. "Sorry I'm late. Hunter needed a change before we left."

"It's fine. I'm just glad you managed to make it." I smile. "Did you want a coffee? I can keep an eye on Hunter."

"No, I don't usually drink coffee. I know, I know," she says in response to the disbelief on Dawn's face. "What kind of mom doesn't drink coffee? I get it all the time."

"Sorry." Dawn smiles. "I just can't get my brain to function without caffeine. Would you like something else?"

"Water, maybe." Amy glances at the line forming at the counter. "I don't know..."

"Here, have mine." I push my glass across the table toward her. She takes a small sip and thanks me.

Dawn stirs an ungodly amount of sugar into her coffee cup. "So, is this a formal meeting?"

"No. I just thought maybe we should get together and talk." I grab a napkin and twist in my hands. "About game night."

"Ah." Dawn takes a sip of her drink before continuing. "I thought that might be it. Is there really anything to talk about? What happened, happened. Not much we can do about it now."

"You kissed my husband." Amy's voice rises sharply.

Dawn's eyes turn stormy as she casts an anxious glance over her shoulder. "Shh! I don't need someone from school finding out what I do in private. That's all I need—some parent complaining to the board. And you kissed mine, too."

"Okay, we all kissed each other's husbands. And we each

kissed," I say quietly. "Was it wrong, what we did? I can't get it out of my head that maybe it was."

"Listen, I don't think it was. So, we got carried away. Big deal. Adults doing adult things." Dawn stirs her coffee.

"Um, I wanted to ask—I don't want to invade your personal lives, but, uh, what happened after everyone left that night?" I chew nervously on the edge of my thumb, thinking that I've gone too far when neither woman answers me. "It's just that, we had, um—it was great. Andrew and I had the best—well, it had been months since we... but that night was... amazing, really."

"Yes," Dawn finally says into the silence. "Lewis was incredibly turned on. And you're right. It was the best sex I've had in ages." She leans back in her chair and sighs.

We both turn and look expectantly at Amy.

"Fine, yes," she says in a small voice. "I just hope I don't get pregnant again." Her hand drops to her stomach.

"So, there we go. We didn't do anything wrong, and we all got a good banging. Now it's over, and we can get on with our lives." Dawn's voice rises until it's in teacher mode.

"Miles wants to do it again," Amy says quickly.

"Miles wants to do what again?" I ask.

"Have another game night. At our house this time." Amy fusses with Hunter, giving him a small bag of cereal O's to snack on. "He says it's only fair that we take turns hosting."

"What I'm hearing is that your husband wants a repeat of spin the bottle. The sex *must* have been amazing." Dawn glances at her watch. "Whatever, I'm up for it if you ladies are." Her gaze drifts to me.

"I just feel like it's cheating, you know?" Amy says. "But Miles is my husband..."

"Hey, don't do anything you don't want to do just because

Miles says so." I lean in to lay my hand over hers. "We'll back you up. Right, Dawn?" I turn to her.

"Yeah, consent is everything." Dawn shakes her head. "No one should feel uncomfortable. Especially in their own home."

"Okay, yeah. I guess I wouldn't mind getting together again. For games." Amy reaches over and wipes at Hunter's chin. "If it's okay with you guys."

"Sure, let's set it up." My stomach flips. I wasn't sure if it was anticipation or dread, but I smiled at Amy. "Sounds like fun."

"Well, all right. See you at game night." Amy stands and gathers pieces of toddler detritus from around Hunter's stroller.

"Right." I force a smile and take another sip of coffee, hoping that my face doesn't appear as conflicted as my mind. "Can't wait."

9

Amy's porch is charming, with flower boxes and rocking chairs and a wooden welcome sign. I imagine two friends sipping iced tea on the chairs, gossiping about the neighborhood. The blooming yellow roses make me wonder if Amy ever sleeps. Somehow, she takes care of four kids, Miles, a large home, and still makes time to garden. I have a regular landscaper and only two children, and I can still barely keep up. I make up my mind to tell her she's doing a great job, just in case she doesn't hear it elsewhere.

"You look great," Andrew murmurs as we climb the steps. His thumb caresses the base of my spine through my silk blouse.

I've added a miniskirt and heels to my outfit tonight and carefully applied Andrew's favorite perfume, the one he got me for Mother's Day last year. I feel pretty. I feel like more than just a mom for the first time in a long while. "Thank you. You don't look bad yourself."

His blue shirt brings out his eyes and his gray slacks accentuate thighs he keeps toned with regular workouts. He winks at me then knocks on the door.

"Hey, hey," Miles booms as he opens the door. He waves us inside and gives a low, appreciative whistle. "Looking good, Petra."

"Thanks." I blush as I turn to my husband, but he's not paying attention.

His gaze is focused on the hallway, and the laughter floating out from a room deep inside the house.

"Follow me." Miles gestures grandly and walks down the hall to the family room.

I study Amy's home, taking in the high-end flooring and chic artwork. This is my first time in her house, and it isn't what I'd imagined. She always seems stressed out, so I'd assumed her home would be equally chaotic. Instead, it's the opposite. This could be the reason she doesn't have much of a social life. She's always working, always looking after the kids or cleaning or cooking. Maybe *that's* why she's stressed. She sets such a high standard for herself. Or maybe Miles sets it.

"Here we are." Miles steps into the room, snags a couple of wine glasses from a tray, and passes them to us. "You guys better catch up."

I take a sip before smiling at Dawn and Amy, who, surprisingly, both wear outfits similar to mine. It seems like I'm not the only one who's decided they liked the attention from last time. I find a place on a cream-colored loveseat—really, cream with kids—and pat the cushion next to me for Andrew to sit. He settles back, crosses his legs at the ankle, and takes a sip of his wine, looking utterly at ease and at home. I try to emulate his casual demeanor.

We chat for a bit, and it's easy to see we're all very aware of why we're here. It's just that no one wants to be the first to come out and say it.

Finally, after Amy has taken the time to pass around a

plate of crudités and Miles has freshened up our drinks, Lewis speaks up. "How about we get a game going?" He grins.

"Sounds good." Miles slaps his thighs and stands. "What are we thinking?" He looks around, waiting for someone to say it first.

"How about charades?" Amy suggests.

Miles sends her a sharp glare, but Dawn speaks up before he can say anything. "Charades sounds good."

"Fine. Charades," Miles concedes.

He fetches paper, and we all quickly write up our phrases and drop them into a small bucket Amy collects from the kitchen. Then we get down to playing. During the game, the men shoot each other looks, and I catch Lewis glancing at his watch a few times before pinning Miles with a stare. If Dawn and Amy notice, they don't say anything, and we just continue playing charades until we've run out of phrases.

There's a lull after the game, with no one really saying much, and Miles gets up and heads into the kitchen.

He returns with an empty wine bottle in one hand and a grin on his face. "Who's ready?"

Andrew turns to me with a smile, his eyebrows raised. "Ready?"

"I guess," I say, unable to prevent an electric thrill from shooting up my spine.

I glance at Dawn and Amy. Dawn's face is neutral, no emotion whatsoever crossing her features. Amy, however, stares down at her feet, and her smooth neck flexes as she swallows whatever she's feeling. She glances up at me and quickly pastes on a smile.

We all move to the floor, forming a haphazard circle in the center of the room. Miles drops the bottle into the middle and gives it a spin.

"Looks like we're ready," Lewis says.

"Wait. Just one more thing." Miles reaches into his pocket and pulls out a small bag. He holds it up, a grin plastered across his face. "Let's make this a real party."

"What is that?" Lewis stands and snatches the bag from Miles, studying it, his brow wrinkling. "Pills? For what?"

Miles takes the bag back and looks around at us, his expression almost triumphant. "Just thought we could all use a little loosening up. That we could party with Molly for a bit." He shrugs.

"Miles, where did you get that?" Amy shuffles away from him.

"One of the guys on the jobsite," he says.

If it's what I think it is, then Miles just brought Ecstasy to his game night. I cast a cautious gaze toward Andrew, wondering what he thinks. I haven't taken drugs since the kids were born, but I was no angel in my late teens. I know Andrew wasn't either, because we were into the same things back then.

"Fuck it," Dawn says. "Why not?"

10

Miles shakes the bag like he's trying to entice a stray cat to him. "Who's first?"

"I'm not sure this is a good idea," Amy says. "What if something goes wrong? The kids—"

"Are with their grandparents tonight." He shrugs. "Besides, what could go wrong? And you should definitely take one. If anyone could use some loosening up, it's you, my darling wife." Miles's words come out in a sneer.

"Amy, you don't have to." I scoot across the floor until I'm next to her. "If you don't, I won't, okay?"

"How about we have a talk in the kitchen? Honey," Miles says through gritted teeth.

Amy glances at me, her eyes wide, before she follows Miles out of the room.

"What do you think, Petra?" Dawn asks. "You ever done Ecstasy before?"

"A couple of times in college, but not for a long time." I fold my arms across my chest. The risks seem so much higher when you're a mom with a life and two kids.

"It's no big deal." Lewis leans over and drapes a hand

across Dawn's thigh. "It just relaxes you a bit. Lots of people do it."

"Do you think Amy's okay?" I ask Dawn, glancing toward the kitchen.

I can just see Miles's broad back through the door. He gestures wildly, but before I can go check on her, Andrew puts a hand on my shoulder and shakes his head.

Amy and Miles return, and while her eyes are red rimmed, she doesn't say anything as she takes a seat on the sofa. Miles pulls out the small bag again, opens it, and offers it to Dawn. With a shrug, she takes one of the pills and pops it into her mouth.

"Why does it taste like rotten peanuts?" Dawn grimaces. "Are there peanuts in it?"

"I hope not. I'm allergic," Miles says, holding out the bag to Lewis.

Lewis follows suit, then Miles offers the bag to me. I reach in and pull out one of the small pills. Andrew does the same. He gives me a reassuring nod and pops the pill into his mouth. I do, too, grimacing at the bitter, salty taste that floods my mouth as I swallow.

Miles walks over to Amy and hands her the bag. I watch, my skin crawling, as, under Miles's scrutiny, she puts the drug delicately into her mouth. Her husband nods his approval, then he flings his head back and tosses one of the pills down his throat.

He claps his hands together. "Let's get this party started!"

We gather back into the circle, the wine bottle in the center, each of us with a fresh drink. Miles puffs up, his voice loud, as he spins the bottle. It wobbles wildly before slowing and spinning to a stop in front of Dawn. Miles smirks and pats his lap, then calls Dawn over to him with a wag of his fingers. Dawn just rolls her eyes and huffs her way across the circle to give him a quick kiss.

Andrew is next, and his spin lands on me. Deep relief washes over me, and I lean toward him before Lewis calls out, "No wait, new rule. You can't kiss your spouse."

"That's stupid," Dawn retorts. "And you can't just go making up new rules in the middle of the game."

"Miles, what do you say? Rule change?" Lewis ignores Dawn as he seeks confirmation from elsewhere.

"Yeah, sure, sounds good to me. Andrew, try again." Miles leans back against the edge of the sofa and flicks his fingers at the bottle. "Spin."

Andrew gives me an unreadable look before moving back to the bottle and giving it another spin. This time, it lands on Amy. She blushes prettily as Andrew moves across the circle toward her. I can't help but notice how her hand curls around the back of his neck when he bends to kiss her.

It doesn't take long before the world softens around the edges. Andrew looks like he's relaxing, sinking into the cushions of the sofa, his head lolling on one of Amy's decorative pillows. I feel like I'm in slow motion when Miles approaches me.

"It landed on you." His voice sounds mellow and syrupy.

His lips land on mine, and they're soft, like bubblegum. I lean into the kiss and close my eyes. It's probably the Ecstasy, but I enjoy my kiss with Miles. He cups my face with both hands then allows them to run through my hair, softly caressing me.

When I open my eyes again, Lewis is kissing me. I'm poured over his lap like paint across a canvas. I pull his mouth off mine and look around blurrily. Dawn and Miles are in one corner of the sofa, wrapped around each other. Lewis pulls my face back to his and kisses me again. My eyes drift shut, and I feel like I'm floating. Maybe it's because Lewis has shifted me, pulled me beneath him. His knee drives between mine, pushing my legs apart. I open my eyes when I feel his fingers sliding up my thigh.

"Wait, wait." I push his hand away just before his fingers slip underneath my panties. "We're just supposed to kiss." I lever myself out from under him and look around, groggy.

Then I see them through a haze, Amy and Andrew. Amy sits on him, her legs straddling his lap, her skirt pushed up around her waist, panties hanging from one ankle. Andrew's hands grip her hips. His pants pool on the floor around his feet.

"Andrew?"

I pull away from Lewis and stumble to my feet. I sway, reaching out, my hands groping the air in front of me as I try to steady myself.

"Andrew?" I say again softly.

Music plays now. *Who put on music?* It drowns out Amy's moans as she fucks my husband. Andrew's eyes are closed, but he's engaged in the sex, his hands roaming my friend's body, his hands on her breasts. He leans forward and kisses her chest.

I turn away. A sob gathers in my throat. Pulling at my clothes, I allow my gaze to trail across the room. Dawn and Miles still kiss in one corner. Her blouse is undone, and one hand reaches down to Miles's fly. Lewis lies back across the sofa, one hand caressing the front of his slacks. I can't believe what's happening. *How did I get pulled into what's amounting to an orgy? Wasn't it just supposed to be a kissing game?* And my husband—I can't even look at him. Grabbing my shoes, I turn my back and walk across the room and out the front door. I pause for a moment on Amy's immaculate porch, slip on my shoes, and walk the few blocks to my house.

Andrew and Amy.

I still can't believe it. The sight of them is etched into the back of my eyelids. *Did either of them think to grab a condom? Did he come inside her? What if he gets Amy pregnant?*

I stop and vomit into someone's rose bush. Thankfully, no one sees, but unless it rains tonight, they'll have a nasty surprise in the morning. Then I carry on walking, enjoying the fresh air on my sticky skin. The Ecstasy hasn't worn off yet. Andrew's infidelity will hit even harder when it does. But by the time I'm home, I'm less groggy and slightly more clear-headed.

I pay the babysitter and send her home before heading upstairs. After a quick check on the children's rooms, I get into the shower and turn the hot water all the way up. Then I stand under the spray until I almost feel sober. I wrap up in my big flannel robe and go downstairs to get a cup of tea. I'm standing at the sink, waiting on the water to heat when I hear the side door open.

Andrew comes into the kitchen. "Petra?" His voice is hoarse.

"Hm." I don't turn to look at him. I'm not sure I can.

"I'm sorry, Petra. I really am." He steps toward me. "We got carried away. It was the drugs."

I give up on the boiling water and get a glass of water from the tap, drinking it all in several large gulps.

"You—you were with Lewis," Andrew starts.

"I didn't fuck Lewis," I say plainly, setting my glass in the sink.

"No, no you didn't. I'm sorry. I guess I just thought we were all having fun. It didn't seem like a big deal at the time. And the drugs and alcohol just made it easier, you know, to make a bad decision."

When I turn around, he's standing there, his shirt untucked and his hair disheveled.

"You crossed a line," I say. "The rules were for kisses. *Kisses!* Chaste little kisses, not coming inside my friend. What the *fuck*, Andrew!"

"I'm so sorry." His voice is heavy and thick. "I'm so, so sorry. I thought we were both on the same page. I saw you with Lewis, and you were really into it. I just thought that was where things were... you know... heading."

He has tears in his eyes, and I can't stand that it's working on me.

"I thought the rules were out the window and it'd moved on. You know how we partied in college."

It's true. We did have an open relationship in college. It lasted almost a year until I asked for monogamy. I'd wanted him all to myself.

He cautiously steps over to me and wraps his arms around my waist. He drops his head to my shoulder, and sobs rack his body. "I couldn't live without you and the kids. Petra, I'm so, so sorry."

I sigh heavily. "I know. Look, I won't say it's okay, but I won't hold it against you either. We all got carried away."

"Will you forgive me?" Andrew asks softly.

"Yes... Maybe. I think so. God, I'm so tired. Let's go to bed and try to forget tonight happened." I turn and go back upstairs, Andrew on my heels.

When he reaches out to catch my hand, I pull away.

After we're in bed, though, I can't seem to take my own advice. I can't forget what I saw. Yes, I'll forgive Andrew, eventually. But I'll never forget. I roll away from Andrew's warm body and wrap my arms around myself, unable to sleep for hours.

11

"Come on, honey. Get your shoes on," I tell Olivia while I wrestle Luca into a jacket. "You don't want to be late, do you?"

"No, Mommy," Olivia chirps.

"No, Mommy," Luca echoes.

It makes me chuckle when Luca copies his big sister. Olivia mostly enjoys playing with her little brother, and I want to hold on to these moments. Soon, they'll be teenagers who act like they hate each other, even though they love each other, and I'll have to deal with that. But right now is the perfect time, and part of me wants to keep it like this for as long as I can.

When Andrew and I first married, I hated the idea of being a stay-at-home mom. But by the time I fell pregnant with Olivia, Andrew's therapy practice—set up with his old college friend, Jules—was taking off. It made sense to give up my lower-paid job in advertising to support him by raising the kids. If I'm honest, even with the tough days, including the ones when Luca throws his shoes at me or smears sweet potato across the walls or when Olivia screams bloody murder, I've never regretted it. I'm sure I could've kept my job and still been a great mom, but having time with them has been a gift. I often feel sorry for Andrew working such long hours, missing out on all this.

"Okay, we're ready. Finally." I toss a tote bag over my shoulder and grab the kids' hands before leading them out the door and down the walk.

I bundle them into my white mom-mobile, my name for the oversized SUV Andrew insisted we buy when we moved here from the city. After the short drive to the library, we pile out of the car and into the wide brick building, pausing to hang up our jackets. Then we head to the children's area for the weekly story time. Today's reader is a lady with bright-red hair and an even brighter sweater. She has a stuffed llama on her lap and several books stacked to the side. She smiles at all the kids, greeting some of them by name. Olivia and Luca pick out their places on the multicolored rug and wait patiently for story time to start.

We're two books in when my phone rings.

I jump then fumble it out of my tote. "Sorry," I mouth to the lady leading story time. I silence my phone quickly then step between the stacks to look at the screen.

It's Amy. It's been two days since game night at her house. Two days since my husband fucked her.

With a glance to make sure the kids are occupied, I step farther into the stacks and answer the phone. "Hello," I whisper.

"Hi," Amy whispers back. "Why are we whispering?"

"I'm at the library. Story time." I keep my voice low. And in my head, I see Amy, bare from the waist down, sitting on my husband.

"Oh, shoot. I forgot about that," she says. "I wanted to call you. I thought we should talk."

"Hmm." I keep my eye on the kids.

"I wanted to apologize," she says. "What I did was wrong." At this, Amy breaks down. Her sobs echo into my ear. "I'm really, really sorry, Petra. I've always wanted us to be friends, like real friends. And now I went and... did what I did. I don't blame you if you hate me."

"Amy, calm down," I say between her blubbers.

"I've never done drugs before, not that that's an excuse, but everything seemed like a dream."

She breaks down again, and I pull the phone away from my ear with a grimace. When I finally put it back, she's quieted down.

"Okay, listen, Amy. I don't blame you," I tell her. "A lot of boundaries got crossed that night. We were all high and drunk."

"But it was wrong," she says, her voice raising. "I'm really not that kind of person."

"I don't think any of us are. But the important thing is that we own up to it and move on. We're all adults. We all made the decision to take the"—I stop and look around—"the drugs," I finish quietly.

"You don't hate me?"

"I don't hate you. And I don't want you to hate yourself. Okay?"

Taking a deep breath, I lean back against one of the stacks, closing my eyes. If I'm honest with myself—and Amy—I don't know how to feel. I don't hate her. I'm shocked by it all, but I don't hate her or blame her. In my mind, Andrew should have stopped it. Amy has never taken an illegal substance in her life—I'm sure of that—but Andrew has. *Why was it I could I stop Lewis before things went too far, but Andrew apparently couldn't?*

Then there's Miles. His wife doesn't even drink coffee, and

he pressured her into dropping ecstasy. *What does that say about him?*

"Okay." She sounds brighter. "I hope—that maybe we can still be friends? I've always admired you, you know. You always seem like you have it together."

I laugh far too loud for a library and slink farther into the shelves. "Hardly. And maybe we can be proper friends. I just need some time to process what happened. All right?"

"Thanks, Petra," Amy says.

"And you know what? It was pretty gutsy of you to call me. Only a person who knows their own mind and doesn't want to compromise their principles would do something like that," I tell her.

"You're too nice to me," Amy says quietly. "Thanks again."

I hang up without saying anything and sneak back to the children's section, easing myself into a child-sized chair while avoiding the steely gaze of the story-time lady.

We get home, and I settle the kids in front of a cartoon with a snack, grab my phone, and head out to the back deck. Glancing to make sure Olivia and Luca are still okay, I slide the glass door shut and pull up Dawn's number before I can change my mind. It rings several times, and I think it's going to voicemail when Dawn picks up.

"Hello," she says.

"Hi, it's Petra," I reply.

"I know." She sounds like she's eating. "Your name came up on the screen, you silly goose. What's up?"

"I got a call from Amy earlier. She was pretty upset about the other night. I just wanted to check on you, see how you're doing." I glance through the door at the kids.

Dawn exhales, and I can tell she's trying to compose herself. "I thought Amy would be upset. She's really not—the other night just isn't the kind of scene where I'd expect to find a person like Amy."

"I guess not. Honestly, I kind of thought the same thing about myself. I mean, when I was younger, maybe I would have been more into it. Andrew and I weren't even exclusive the first year we dated," I confess. "But even then, I didn't do anything, uh, in a group setting."

Dawn laughs. "I guess I can see that about you. Back to Amy, though, did she say anything else about that night?"

"No, she just apologized for sleeping with my husband. Why? What else happened?" I pace across the deck, the boards creaking beneath my weight.

Dawn remains silent for so long that I check if our call has disconnected.

Finally, she says, "It got a little crazy after you and Andrew left."

"Crazy how?" I cross to one of the deck chairs we have covered for the winter and sit. "What happened?"

"Well, I wound up in a threesome with Lewis and Miles," Dawn confesses. "It just kind of happened. I'm not even sure where Amy was, but I'm sure she knows about it. I don't know what to say to her."

"That is... crazy." I'm so shocked I don't know what to say.

"Crazy," Dawn repeats.

I'm quiet as I digest what Dawn just told me. *How could we have let it get this far? Was it really the drugs, or did they simply allow us—a group of parents and professionals—to act out fantasies boiling just below the surface?* Maybe underneath the big suburban houses, cookouts, PTAs, yoga classes, and SUVs, we're all just sexually repressed housewives looking for the first opportunity to remedy our boredom.

"Do you think I should call Amy?" Dawn interrupts my thoughts.

"Actually, no. I think maybe we all need to take a break," I say. "No more game nights, no meeting up for drinks or coffee, nothing. This is too much. We all have too much to lose if this becomes public. So, let's just—take a break."

"You win the award for the most adult among us. But you're right." She sighs. "We crossed some lines. And all this because you and I had that drunken kiss."

I rub the chill from my arms. "Yeah. I can't believe it."

An awkward silence follows before Dawn says, "Okay, well, I guess I'll see you around."

"I guess so."

With that, I hang up and head back inside to snuggle with the kids and spend the afternoon watching cartoons.

12

"Do you have your backpack?" I hold Luca by one hand and slide my purse over my shoulder with the other while directing Olivia to gather her school things. "Also, don't forget we have to bake cookies tonight for the bake sale."

"Chocolate chip!" Luca shouts as he tries to tug his hand out of mine.

I hold tight, knowing that if I let him, he'll dash off, and I'll have to play an impromptu game of hide-and-seek before I get the kids to school.

"Fine, chocolate chip." I tug him along.

"I want oatmeal," Olivia says firmly.

"We'll do both if you two will just get moving," I say to avoid an argument.

I finally wrangle the kids down the steps and driveway to the car. I help them hop into the back seat and buckle in. It's only when I walk around to the driver's side that I see a large scratch beginning at the front bumper and extending all the way to the rear. I trace it with my finger. Definitely a scratch. And a deep one at that. *What the hell?*

I don't have time to investigate, though, because I have to get the kids to school before they're late. I jump in and back down the driveway.

"Hey, monkeys, Mommy has a question." I study the children in the rearview mirror. "Did you notice a scratch on Mommy's car when you were playing outside yesterday?"

"No, Mommy," Olivia says.

Luca echoes her.

"Did you make a scratch on Mommy's car when you were playing?" I glance back at them.

"Not me," Luca pipes up.

"I didn't, Mommy," Olivia says. "Can we have white chocolate chips? I changed my mind, Mommy!"

"Hmm," I mutter, distracted by the scratch.

The kids aren't good enough at lying to be that nonchalant about it. Besides, I saw how deep the scratch was, and I don't think either child would have the strength. Now I have to take the car to the shop. It looked suspiciously like a key or some other sharp metal object was used. Something about it seemed deliberate. Almost like a message. *But why?*

The kids start arguing over cookies, and Olivia flings her backpack to the floor in a fit. I sigh as I pull into the school lot, grateful that I'll have a few childless hours to do my errands for the day.

After I walk Luca to his class and assure Olivia I'll buy ingredients for both flavors of cookies, I head back to the car, stopping for a couple of minutes to study the scratch again. I make a mental note to call a few paint shops when I get home for a quote to repair the damage.

I'm only a few blocks away from the school when I notice the black SUV. At first, I don't think anything of it. It's the suburbs. Every mom in town drives an SUV of some sort. But then I notice that the car takes the same turns for several minutes. I shake off the feeling of apprehension settling between my shoulders. *Don't be paranoid,* I tell myself. I turn down a street I wouldn't normally take and glance into the rearview mirror. Sure enough, the black SUV turns in behind me. My heart leaps into my throat, and I have to stop myself from punching the gas and speeding through the neighborhood.

I'm being followed. I'm sure of it. And the scratch on my car can't be a coincidence. *But why? And who?* I contemplate slowing down enough to see if I can get a look at who's driving the black SUV, but I'm not sure if that would be dangerous. Instead, I take the next turn and head toward the shops on the opposite end of town. The car keeps pace with me, following each turn I make. When I pull into the grocery store lot, the black SUV shoots past me and continues down the street, disappearing before I can park my car. I sit for a few minutes, watching to see if the SUV comes back, but it never does. I finally head inside, glancing over my shoulder with every step, afraid that I'll be run down in the market parking lot.

Once inside the store, I notice my fingers trembling. My body is cold all over. The scratch and the strange SUV have really shaken me. I spend an absurd amount of time walking each aisle and inspecting the specials on every endcap. Part of me doesn't want to leave the safety of this building with its witnesses and bright lights. I take my time choosing candy chips for the cookies, getting not only milk and white chocolate but butterscotch as well. Finally, after I've circled the store for the third time, I check out. I swallow my nerves, gather my shopping bags, and head out to the lot. My heart sinks when I study it. *Why do so many people in this town drive black SUVs?* Taking a deep breath, I head across the concrete parking area toward my car. Which isn't there.

"What?" *Am I in the wrong lane?* I walk one lane over and look around. Finally, I pull my keys out of my purse and hit the alarm button on my key fob. Nothing. No shrieking alarm to help me pinpoint my car. It takes a few minutes before the realization sets in. My car's been stolen.

I head back into the store, concerned for my safety, and go to the first staff member I see. "I was just in here, and my car has been stolen. Can I stand in here and make a few calls, please?"

The thin guy with ginger hair smiles sympathetically. "Sure. Do you want to step into the back?"

I consider it, but then think I might be best out here with more people around. "No thanks."

I call the police and wait next to my bags sitting on the ground. My feet are numb by the time the police arrive, but it's a relief to see them. I haven't called Andrew yet. I'm not sure why. Maybe part of me feels like I've made a mistake, and I don't want the embarrassment of admitting it to anyone I know, not even my husband.

The officer walks into the store, his boots heavy on the linoleum. "Mrs. Ross?"

I nod.

In his mid-forties, he's slim and bearded. "I'm Officer Denton. Can we sit somewhere and chat?"

A flustered-looking man approaches. His eyes flit from the store to the police officer and back again. "Perhaps you'd like to use my office?"

It's more than a suggestion. He wants us out of the way of customers. I grab my shopping bags and follow him to a small room at the back of the store. Officer Denton gestures for me to sit.

"Perhaps someone could get Mrs. Ross a cup of coffee." He smiles at the store manager.

I'm grateful for that. While I'm not particularly thirsty, the fact that the officer is thoughtful enough to suggest it puts me at ease.

"All right. In your own time, Mrs. Ross."

I launch into the day's events, starting with the mysterious scratch and ending with the stolen car. The store manager returns promptly with a cup of coffee, but I let it cool as I talk. Denton nods occasionally and jots notes in a small notebook he pulled from his shirt pocket. When I tell him about the SUV that followed me, he's quite dismissive of it.

"It's a small town with limited turns," he says. "I'm not saying I don't believe you, just that it could easily be a coincidence."

"I guess," I admit. "But you have to admit, paired with the deliberate scratch, it's—"

He holds up a hand. "You don't know it's deliberate. Again, I'm not dismissing your concerns, just stating facts."

"What about my car, though. Do you think you'll find it?"

"Best advice I can give you is to contact your insurance company. Chances are, even if we find it, it'll be trashed." The cop shrugs and shoves his notebook back into his pocket. He pulls out a business card and passes it to me. "We'll let you know if we find anything. And of course, call us if it shows up. Anything else you can remember?"

"No, I think I've told you everything." I glance at the floor, where my shopping bags are piled around my feet. "Thanks for your time."

"No problem." He leaves the room quickly.

I can tell he's already moved on to something else entirely. I guess a suburban mom losing her car isn't a huge priority.

"Do you need a ride home?" the store manager asks as I'm about to leave.

I pause, standing in the doorway, realizing I hadn't even thought about getting home.

"I'll call my husband." I take out my phone, then I burst into tears.

13

"Oh my god, are you all right?" The store manager shoves a handful of paper towels at me and stands, wringing his hands.

"Yeah, I'm fine. It's just been a lot. But I guess I should call my husband." I mop my wet cheeks with the rough towels. I take a few deep breaths to calm myself then call Andrew. He doesn't answer.

Glancing at the time, I know he's in his office, so I call the business line, aggravated when his office phone goes straight to voicemail. I wait a couple of minutes then call his cell phone again. After several calls go unanswered, I resist the urge to toss my phone across the room.

The manager hovers, his feet shifting back and forth. "Can you call anyone else? You could get an Uber maybe?"

I glance at the bags piled around my feet. Taking an Uber with all these shopping bags is the last thing I want to do. I scroll through my phone contacts, trying to find someone who might be available. The only person I can find is Amy. Though we'd all agreed to take a break from one another, this is an emergency. Fuck it. She owes me. I hit the call button, and she answers on the second ring. As soon as I explain my predicament, she offers to pick me up.

"I'll be there in twenty minutes," she says.

Thirty minutes later, I load my bags into the back of Amy's silver minivan and brush crushed cookies off the seat while her youngest babbles in the back.

"I can't believe someone stole your car." Amy shakes her head as she steers us out of the lot. "I mean, stuff like that just doesn't happen here." She reaches back with one hand and hands Hunter a sippy cup without taking her eyes off the road. "Things have just been really insane around here lately."

I feel her looking at me from the corner of her eye.

"They have," I say cautiously. I get the feeling she's not talking about my car.

"I mean, just look at us and what happened." We roll to a stop at a red light, and Amy turns to me. "I'm still sorry for what happened with Andrew. I know you said you forgave me, but I'm not sure I can forgive myself. At least, not yet."

"Try not to think about it," I say, my gaze resolutely forward. "The lights have changed."

She puts her hands back on the wheel and pulls forward. "Um, it's kind of hard for me to forget. Miles keeps bringing it up."

"Is he angry with you?" I ask. "Because he's the one who brought the drugs."

"No. Believe it or not, he's not angry. It's the opposite. Miles wants an open relationship now. He thinks the game nights have helped us." Amy lets out a high, false laugh.

"Oh," I say slowly as we turn into our neighborhood. "You have to be very careful with that, Amy."

"I haven't said yes, yet. I told him I'd think about it." She turns the van onto our street.

"What do you think about it, though? Just pull straight up." I point to the drive. "I can go in through the kitchen door."

Amy guides the minivan up my driveway and pulls to a stop. She puts the car in park and turns to me. "I think that if it's going to happen, it's better to be with friends. A small group of people we trust."

"That sounds like Miles talking," I say. "You should give it more thought. Don't forget it's your decision, too."

"You sound like you've had experience with this," Amy says.

"In a manner of speaking. When we first started dating, Andrew and I weren't exclusive. In fact, it took a year before we finally agreed to it being just us," I confess. I rustle around on the floorboards and snag my purse from under my feet.

"What happened?" Amy asks with interest.

"It's hard dating other people while you're in a relationship. You have a lot of people's feelings to consider, not just your own. You don't want to mess with someone else's life, you know. Communication is key."

"Okay, but what aren't you telling me?" Amy wiggles a finger at me.

"Well, for it to happen, you can't have secrets. Honesty is paramount. And someone will always get jealous. That's what ended it for us," I acknowledge. "We both started to get jealous of each other's dates. That's when we knew it had to end."

"I think, if it were just our group, you know, the carpool moms, maybe I wouldn't get jealous," Amy says. "I trust you and Dawn."

"Do you trust your husband?" I ask pointedly.

When she doesn't answer, I gather my bags and tell her

goodbye, hoping that she'll take our conversation to heart and consider what her husband proposed.

I drag my bags into the kitchen and put away my shopping. While I refill the coffee pot—because it's too early for wine, so I might as well caffeinate—Andrew calls. He brushes me off when I ask him why it took so long to return my call by telling me he was with a client.

"How could this even happen? What were you doing? God, our insurance will go up." Andrew's voice borders on accusatory.

"Oh, I don't know, buying food for your children. Guess I should have realized a car thief was in the parking lot," I snap. "And yes, I'm fine. Totally not traumatized or anything."

"Did you lock the car? Opportunity and all that," he says. "Criminals take the path of least resistance."

"Damn it, Andrew, yes. No. I don't know, maybe. If you can't say something comforting right now, how about we end this conversation? I have to figure out a way to get the kids from school." I grab a mug from a cabinet and slam the door shut. "You're not being helpful."

"Fine," he replies, his voice tight. "I'll pick up the kids from school. How's that for being helpful?"

"It's literally the least you could do." I pour a cup of coffee and search for the sugar.

"Just a thanks would do. Or is that too much to ask?" Andrew snaps.

"You know what? I've had too rough of a day to stroke your ego. You'll pick up the kids because they're your kids, too. I'll see you this afternoon." I tap my phone off and toss it onto the counter with a shake of my head.

What am I angry about, and who am I angry with? Myself, for starting this whole mess by kissing Dawn? Andrew, for crossing a line we hadn't agreed to cross? Amy, for crossing that line with him?

I think back to what Amy said, that Miles thought an open relationship would help their marriage. I wonder if Andrew would agree. I think he probably would. *And what about me?* Today was awful and confusing but it made me realize how stuck I am in this suburban rut. Back in my twenties, I wouldn't have burst into tears over a stolen car, and Andrew wouldn't have snapped at me about it. Maybe I need some freedom, too. Maybe I just need to understand that the rules have changed. Maybe being in an open relationship would help us—as long as it's mutual and with people we trust. I sip my coffee, wishing it were wine, and wonder who I can trust.

14

I stumble out of bed and blearily make my way to the bathroom. I haven't slept well. Having a car stolen, being followed, and considering an open relationship with their husband will do that to a person. I peer into the bathroom mirror and rub the sleep from my eyes. I just splashed cold water across my face when the smell hits me.

It's rank and smells like a petting zoo I took the kids to a few months ago. I open the toilet lid and peer inside, thinking maybe the pipes have backed up. When I don't find anything, I check under the sink then in the shower. Still nothing.

"What the hell is that?" Andrew wanders in and looks around. "Smells like straight sewage."

"I don't know." I check the wastebasket in the corner then sniff the clothes hamper.

Andrew gives me a look then immediately checks everything I've already checked in the bathroom. I resist rolling my eyes as I walk back into the bedroom. The smell grows stronger here. I search under the bed before picking up Andrew's shoes he discarded near the door and checking the bottoms. Nothing.

I sniff and follow my nose. When I find myself near the window, I draw the curtains and unlock it, then push it open. The smell makes me gag.

It's so strong, drifting in on the early-morning air. I shove the window shut and turn to Andrew. "It's coming from outside."

Shrugging into a robe and stepping into my slippers, I head downstairs and cross to the front door, Andrew on my heels. As I pull it open, I immediately slap a hand over my mouth and nose. I follow the scent down the walk to the driveway, finally ending up at the street.

It's a huge pile of dung. Huge. Stacked up a good few feet and just dumped in the middle of the road. I don't even know where it could have come from. *A farm, maybe?* Despite the stench, my jaw drops. It sits in the street, the stench radiating, filling the neighborhood that normally smells of cut grass and bougainvillea. The neighbor from across the street hurries down his drive, his face wrinkled in disgust.

"What in the hell?" He skirts the pile and walks over to me. "You know anything about this?"

"Nope," I say. "Only that it's making my entire house smell like a sewage plant."

A few more neighbors join us, including Dawn and Lewis.

"That is the biggest pile of shit I've ever seen." Lewis screws up his nose. "Is it from an animal, do you think?"

"Let's hope so," I mutter. "What should we do about this?"

"Well, it's too big for a doggie poop bag," someone says with a laugh.

"I think we should call the police. This is vandalism," Dawn says after a few seconds. "Unless we have a dinosaur roaming the neighborhood, someone put this here on purpose."

"Good idea," I say. "Andrew, do you have your phone? Could you call the non-emergency line?"

He nods and steps away, his phone to his ear.

"What should we do?" asks an older woman from down the block. "We have to get it out of here. Isn't it a biohazard or something?"

"We need to hire a professional," Dawn replies. "Anybody here on the HOA board? I think it's something they'd cover from their funds."

"I think you two should take care of this." The older woman points to me and Dawn. "You seem to know what to do. I wouldn't know where to begin."

Dawn and I look at each other. It seems that despite our agreement to take a break from one another, the universe has conspired to bring us together. Albeit in the smelliest way imaginable.

Dawn sighs. "Looks like it's you and me, kid. Nothing but a pair of shit stirrers."

I move to stand beside her, cracking a half smile. "I guess after the police make a report, we need to locate a sanitation service to remove it and disinfect the area."

The rest of the neighbors nod then wander back toward their homes, relieved that they don't have to deal with the giant pile of poop scenting our street. Even Andrew, after telling us the police are on their way, goes back inside and leaves me and Dawn standing on the curb.

"Why don't you come in?" I ask Dawn. "We can look for some sanitation disposal companies and get away from the smell."

"Sure," Dawn replies. "Got any coffee?"

"I can get some going." I lead her up the driveway.

Inside, I quickly get the coffee pot going and pull out the

laptop so we can search a few disposal companies. We make a few calls while the coffee brews.

"I think this looks like the best company." Dawn taps the notebook we used to write down information from our calls. "It's not the cheapest option, but they can come out the quickest. We need to get that mess out of the road."

"I'll call the HOA president, make sure they can pay for it," I reply. "I wonder if anyone saw anything. Maybe on a doorbell camera or something like that?"

"I'm sure the police will go over that with everyone," Dawn says.

"I wouldn't be so sure. They weren't exactly the most helpful when my car got stolen."

I top off my coffee cup and wiggle the carafe at Dawn, offering her more. She nods, and I refill her cup.

"Maybe we should go ask a few people ourselves."

"That's not a bad idea." Dawn blows across the top of her steaming cup. "After the police take their statements and we change clothes"—Dawn gestures from me to her in our robes—"we'll go together and talk to a few neighbors."

"Sounds like a plan. Oh, looks like the police are here." I leave Dawn sitting at my kitchen counter and answer the door.

After dealing with the police, Dawn heads back to her house to change and I call Andrew to let him know we're heading out into the neighborhood.

"It's just for half an hour or so," I tell him, annoyed that I even have to ask. "If you give them an iPad, they won't bother you." I sit on the bottom stair putting on my shoes.

"Why don't you let the police take care of it?" Andrew

stands over me, his arms crossed. "I don't see why you have to go out and play detective with your girlfriend."

"She's not my girlfriend," I mutter, my face flushing at the implication. "And the police have done all they're going to do."

"Fine, half an hour. I have things to do, too. I need to go to the office." He walks out of the hallway, his body tense.

"I bet you do," I say softly. I consider going after him, reminding him that I didn't have these children on my own but it would just lead to another fight. Instead, I finish tying my shoes and head out to meet Dawn at the end of the street.

We go from house to house, knocking on every door and asking our neighbors if they remember seeing anything suspicious this morning before we discovered the pile of dung. Luckily, the sanitation company has already been out, so the only smell on the street now is woodsmoke from someone's fireplace and the faint scent of disinfectant from the removal company. As we walk from house to house, I tell Dawn about being followed the day my car was stolen.

"Do you think this has anything to do with that?" she questions. "I mean, it was right in front of your house."

"It was also in front of the Clatterbucks'," I reply. "But I don't know. It does seem like I'm being harassed or something." I stop in the middle of the sidewalk. "I can't think of any reason someone would do any of those things."

"And I can't believe only one person saw anything that might be useful. Do you think the truck Helen saw was the same one that followed you?" Dawn looks up and down the street like it might appear just because we're talking about it.

"I don't know. I'm pretty sure it was an SUV, not a truck, that followed me." I put my thumbnail in my mouth and chew. "I'm not sure what to think anymore. Things have been strange around here lately."

"Speaking of strange," Dawn says, "guess what I've been thinking about doing?"

"Hmm, what?" I keep chewing on my nail, watching the street turn orange as the sun sets.

"I'm thinking about hosting another game night."

I drop my hand and face Dawn. "Funny, you're the second person who's mentioned that to me."

"Amy?" Dawn questions.

"Yup, and now, you. Amy and I had a very illuminating conversation when she picked me up the other day. What happened to us taking a break from each other?" I tap my foot quickly on the pavement.

"Seems like it's not working out that well," Dawn admits. "Lewis has even talked about, you know, swapping." She slides me a look from the corner of her eye.

"Funny, Amy was saying something pretty similar the other day. I'm not sure, Dawn. The last game night got out of hand."

"I've been thinking about that. It might be better, well, if we were all game, and of course, if we set rules and expectations beforehand. That way everyone would know exactly where the lines are." Dawn glances down the street as a car passes. "I think we missed the element of communication last time."

"Oh, we definitely did. And I think we were all too high to give informed consent. The rules need to be arranged while sober." I start down the sidewalk toward my house, leaves crunching under my feet. "Wow, that feels ridiculous to say. I'm not exactly twenty-one, am I?" I tut to myself. "Are we too old for these... shenanigans?"

"We're not dead, Petra. If it's what we want to do, why not? So, what do you think?" Dawn grabs my hand. Her thumb swipes over my palm so quickly, I almost miss it, but my heartbeat picks up from the touch.

"I—would have to think about it." I pull my hand away and immediately miss the warmth of Dawn's fingers. "It's getting cold. I think we should get inside."

"Talk to you soon?" Dawn asks.

"Yes, we'll talk soon."

I stop at the end of my drive and watch as Dawn climbs the stairs to her porch before I turn and go inside my house. And I think about how Dawn's hand felt on mine.

15

The kids run circles around me, singing a nonsense rhyming song while I try to vacuum. Little feet thunder through the room, dodging the head of the vacuum, landing on sofa cushions. Andrew will be home shortly, and I don't want him to see the trail of dirt Luca tracked across the foyer when he came in from digging in the backyard. It's bad enough that the landscaper will need to fill in several holes Luca managed to make while my back was turned.

I barely hear the doorbell over all the noise. Catching a glimpse of myself in a mirror, I try to smooth the sloppy bun sitting on top of my head. It's useless, so I quickly brush the dust off my yoga pants and answer the door.

A handsome, young delivery guy stands on the porch, holding a vase full of hydrangea blooms and white roses. I smell the flowers before he even hands them to me. Acutely aware that I look like I've been dragged through a bed of sticks, I take the flowers and quickly shut the door behind me. The kids are still traipsing through the house, singing their song, so I take the flowers into the kitchen and set them on the counter, searching for a card.

"Who are those from?" Andrew comes in from the garage, and I glance at the clock. He's late. Again. I bite my tongue and keep searching for a card.

"I thought maybe they were from you." I pluck a small white envelope from the center of the blooms. "But I guess not."

"It's not like it's our anniversary." Andrew tosses his coat over a chair and heads to the refrigerator. He grabs a beer and moves closer, studying the flowers. "Well, who're they from?"

My chest tightens. *What if they're from the person who followed me in the SUV? Or who stole my car? Or left a huge pile of dung outside our house?* I rip the small envelope open.

"They're from Lewis," I say, relieved but also nervous in a different way.

"Lewis? What?" Andrew plucks the card from my fingers and flips it over, reading the note. "Game night, huh?"

"It seems that way. Dawn did mention it the other day." I pull the vase to me, fluffing the flowers and rearranging a few of the stems. "We don't have to go." I take the card from him and read it again. "'Come prepared to party.' We both know that means one thing."

Andrew settles onto a counter stool and studies the flowers. "What do you think about it?" He flicks one of the buds.

"About... game night? Uh, well, we know what'll happen if we go. That's pretty obvious." I wave the card at Andrew. "Are you asking me if I want to go? Do you want to go?"

"I wouldn't object," he says in a noncommittal voice. "I'm worried, though, after you ran out last time. Is it something you want?"

"Well, Dawn and I were talking about it," I start.

Andrew laughs. "Oh, you guys have already talked about it? Anything left for you and me to discuss?" He reaches over and pulls me toward him, wrapping his arms around my waist. "But really, if we consider this, we have to talk. I don't want you to feel obligated to go, and I don't want you to be uncomfortable there."

I'm quiet for a moment.

He continues, "You know, I've counseled a few couples who found an open relationship saved their marriage. Some even became a thruple and made it work. The idea of monogamy is more modern than we think it is—"

"You want the truth?" I interrupt, sensing a lecture coming on.

"Always, sweetheart. Be honest with me. I won't be mad if you say no." He presses a kiss to my temple.

"I'm—kind of intrigued. To maybe try again? Only this time knowing what we're getting into." I swallow as I wait for his reaction.

"You trying to say you're excited by the thought of being with another man?" His voice is even.

"Yes," I confess.

"And what about seeing me with another woman? How would that make you feel?" he asks gently.

"It was just a shock last time. We hadn't agreed on anything. We were supposed to be playing spin the bottle. So yeah, it was jarring, to say the least. But if I know what we're going into, if I know that you'll be with someone else, maybe it will be different." As I say the words, I know I mean it. And the thought of us both being with someone else does excite me.

My insides warm as I think about it, and I know Andrew can tell because he chuckles and runs a hand over my hip.

"We need to set our expectations before we go. Lay down some rules."

"So, are you saying yes?" Andrew's fingers make slow circles over my hip.

"I'm saying yes, as long as we're honest with each other, we communicate our needs, and we make sure we're both comfortable." I lean into Andrew.

"Okay, we'll give it another try." He grins.

"Oh, don't make it sound like you're doing it just for me." I laugh. "I know you're looking forward to this, too. I'm just not sure which of my friends you want to fuck the most."

"Hey, I'm just a red-blooded man." He pulls me forward and gives me a quick kiss. "But if, for any reason, we decide it's not for us, then we leave. Agreed?"

"Agreed. But maybe we need something, like a—"

"A safe word?" he suggests.

"Yeah, like that."

"Okay, let's pick a safe word," he says.

"All right, how about rainstorm?" I reply.

"Rainstorm? I guess I could work that into a conversation. Rainstorm it is." Then he pulls me closer and kisses me again.

I can't help but replay something Andrew said to me. *You're excited by the thought of being with another man?* I'd said yes, and I'd thought I'd meant it. But I didn't. Not by the thought of being with another *man* anyway.

16

"You look gorgeous." Dawn's eyes crawl over me as she ushers us into the house.

My short skirt flares around my thighs as I walk. My heels make my legs look miles long. My hair is up, exposing the column of my neck, and my lips are painted a glistening red. I feel sexy.

"Thank you. So do you." The words sound strangely formal leaving my mouth. My heart pounds. Now that I know what the evening will entail, nerves flutter in my stomach.

She does look great. Dawn's revealing romper plunges low in the front and accentuates the slope of her hips, barely covering her generous curves. I can't help but watch her sway as she leads us to the family room.

Miles and Amy have already settled on the sofa, Miles with a drink in hand and Amy curled against his side. She smiles when she sees us and gets up to greet me with a hug.

"Oh, you both look so great. I wish I'd dressed fancier." Amy pulls at her skirt.

I smile and tell her that her white wrap dress makes her look like an angel. She blushes at the compliment.

Miles and Andrew do that handshake, shoulder-clap thing men do with each other before turning to us. Miles has obviously already had a few drinks. He talks at a louder volume than usual and seems excited. He keeps telling Andrew how he's looked forward to this as he eyes Dawn's cleavage.

We don't get a chance to chat much because Lewis comes in from the kitchen. He carries a silver tray with an empty wine bottle, a carefully arranged line of small, rainbow-colored pills, and an equally colorful display of condoms. It's almost ritualistic. He sets the tray down and claps his hands.

"Okay, we've talked about it." He gestures to Dawn. "And I'm sure you guys have, too. We think we should set a few rules. That okay?" He looks around for our agreement. "All right, first things first, since you're here, and we're all sober right now, we assume that means you consent to what's happening tonight, right?"

We all nod.

"Then let's run through a few guidelines. First, if you're uncomfortable, let your partner know. We all realize no means no here. Second, this is a swap. You have to go with someone other than your own wife or husband. Third, no jealousy. We're all adults here, and we know what we're getting into. And fourth, this does not continue outside these walls. Just because it's okay in the group doesn't mean it's okay for you to meet up alone. It all stays in the group. And lastly, keep this between us. Not everyone needs to know what we've been up to." He looks around, making sure we all agree. "Let's get this party started then."

He grabs the tray and offers it to us. We all take one of the colored pills. I roll mine back and forth between my fingers, wondering if I really want to take it. I turn to Andrew, but his eyes are on Amy. I pop the pill into my mouth.

Let's get this party started, I think.

Andrew caresses my arm. "Are you okay?"

"Sure." I sip my wine, chasing the pill's bitterness from my mouth.

On the floor, Lewis sets up the bottle. My heart beats harder. *Will I have to sleep with whoever this lands on?* It could be the wine, or the pill, but my body suddenly feels red-hot. *Could I really have sex with Miles knowing he's an overbearing husband? What about Amy?* She's pretty, but I find nothing attractive about her.

I shake the thoughts away. I'm overthinking it. Tonight is about fun. When the air around me softens, melting into a pile of sugary mellowness, I let it take me. I'm barely aware of moving across the room toward Lewis after the spun bottle points toward me. Everything is hazy in a pleasant way, and I dissolve across Lewis's lap to let him kiss me. The kiss goes on and on.

Lewis explores my body, pushing my blouse open to slide his large hand inside. He's almost familiar now, and I let him work his fingers up along my ribs until they brush across my lace-covered breasts. The movement jolts me out of my haze for a moment. I look around the room. Dawn and Miles are entwined on the other side of the sofa, their attention on only each other. Which means the other couple is Andrew and Amy. I let Lewis kiss up the side of my neck while I watch them from the corner of my eye.

Do those two seem to gravitate toward each other for some reason? Does Andrew like her petite frame, her small, birdlike motions, or her soft brown hair? Maybe it's her innate submissiveness that pulls him to her. *And what is it about my husband that Amy likes? Is he kind to her? Is he generous and giving?* A small barb of jealousy spears me, but I try to ignore it. It's not like I can say anything, given that I seem to pair up with

Lewis. I look away and try to think about what Lewis is doing instead.

Lewis pulls his mouth from my cleavage and looks at me, his mouth glistening.

"Let's go find somewhere more private," he slurs a little.

I nod yes, and he stands and takes my hand. This is it. If I don't pull away now, then there's no going back. I glance over at Amy and Andrew again. Their bodies are entwined. She's almost naked. I let Lewis lead me away.

We stumble up the stairs and into what I suspect is Lewis and Dawn's bedroom. A king-sized bed dominates the space, but Lewis pulls me across the room and into the closet. The large walk-in is so big, it could be used as another bedroom. Rows of clothing run the length, and a lit vanity anchors one end. Lewis drops into a tufted blue velvet chair that Dawn probably uses to put her shoes on every morning. He pulls me onto his lap and shoves his hands up my blouse again.

I let him do whatever he wants. His hands wander over me, pushing aside whatever clothing gets in his way. When I try to help him with his clothes, he moves my hands and does it himself, like I'm doing something wrong. So I just let him do it himself.

Lewis's mouth sucks at my skin, leaving small red marks across my chest. I lean my head back and try to find the haze that took me earlier. I find it easier if I don't look at him. I try not to think about Andrew or the fact that the man with his hands in my panties isn't my husband. When Lewis pushes me to the floor, I tumble back willingly.

It's different with this man. His weight isn't what I'm used to. The feel of his skin is foreign. I let him spread my legs and settle between them, and when he pushes into me, I concentrate on the feeling and shove away the thoughts that it's Lewis. I even keep my eyes closed when he turns me over and pulls me onto my knees.

His breath comes out harsher and harsher, rasping through the air by my neck. His fingers clench my thighs so hard, I'm sure they'll leave a mark. Before I realize what's happening, Lewis collapses on me, pushing us both to the ground. The carpet is rough against my cheek. I feel his weight move away, and I stay where I am, my skirt pushed up and my blouse unbuttoned. He smacks me lightly on my rear.

"I'm going down to get some water," he announces. Then he gets up and walks out of the closet, leaving me lying there among his wife's sweaters and dresses.

I don't know how long I lay on the floor. Time moves in funny ways, thanks to the ecstasy, but eventually, I stand up and straighten my clothes. I use Dawn's vanity mirror to check my face. It's flushed, but I can't do anything about it. I take a deep breath, try to shake off any thoughts about what just happened, and walk out into the bedroom.

Dawn is sitting on the edge of the bed.

17

Dawn pats the bed next to her. I make my way over and gingerly settle onto the edge, and we sit for a few minutes in silence.

"Nice closet," I crack.

She laughs.

"Sorry I fucked your husband in it."

She laughs again, and it becomes infectious. We flop back onto the bed, still grinning.

Dawn rolls onto her side and props herself up on one arm. "Weird, isn't it? I should feel jealous about someone being with Lewis, but I don't."

"I am," I admit. "About Andrew, I mean. Just a smidge. It's easier than I thought it would be, though. So, what are you doing up here?"

"Looking for you," she says.

"Oh?" Nerves coil in my gut.

"I slept with Miles," she says after a few seconds of silence.

"What was it like?" I ask.

"Weird," she says. "Over pretty quickly."

I nod. "Well, he was awfully excited before Lewis even spun the bottle."

Dawn laughs. "I know, right?"

I pause for a moment. "I can't imagine Miles being your type. He's such a..." I try to find a polite way of putting it.

"Pig?" she suggests.

I nod.

"I don't like him or the way he treats my friend," she says. "But I don't think Amy has the strength to leave him yet, and he certainly seems hellbent on pressuring her into this swapping thing." She sighs. "I don't know, I figured if I kept him busy, he might feel like he got what he wants and ease off her a bit. You know? Take one for the team and all that."

"God, I never thought of it like that," I admit. "Maybe you're right. I want to kick him out of the group so badly, but then we wouldn't be able to keep an eye on Amy and make sure she's safe."

Dawn nods.

We let that hang for a moment, then I ask, "So, why were you looking for me?"

"Well, I saw you head up here with Lewis, and I... well, I *did* sort of feel jealous. But not... not for the right reasons. Not for the reason that would make me a good wife." Her brown eyes flick up to mine.

"What do you mean?"

"I don't care who Lewis fucks. He can sleep with my entire hot yoga class, for all I care. But thinking about him touching you makes me want to slice off his fingers." She lifts her hands toward the ceiling in exasperation. "It's *insane*, I know, but I can't stop thinking about that night on the dance floor with the Spice Girls playing then that ballad and—"

Without thinking, I lunge forward, snaking my arms around Dawn's neck to pull her closer. Our mouths collide, heat and want meshing together. She lets out a soft moan, and her fingers tangle in my hair. Dawn's lips travel across my skin from my lips to my neck and back. And when I do the same to her, she tastes like salt and sugar. My mind rushes back to those tequila shots before our first kiss. It makes heat rush through me like adrenaline coursing through my veins.

Dawn rolls me onto my back and settles herself over me, holding her weight off me. Her eyes are questioning, and instead of saying yes, I just kiss her again, hopeful that she'll understand. When her hands trace my body, it's nothing like when Lewis did. Or even Andrew. Dawn's touches are light, fluttering, like butterfly wings. I mirror her every move. If she caresses my face, I caress hers. We move in unison, silken skin against silken skin.

Dawn moves down my body, discarding pieces of clothing as she goes. Her mouth floats across every dip and curve. I stiffen when she parts my legs. She stops and looks up at me from between my thighs. Her fingers graze the most intimate part of me, and I melt into the bed. And when her tongue touches me, I disappear into an abyss of pleasure.

Afterward, Dawn doesn't disappear like Lewis did. She leads me to the bathroom, helps me wash and towel off, planting kisses on my face the entire time. She finds my skirt and blouse and smooths the wrinkles before helping me step into them. Finally, she stands behind me, her chin resting on my shoulder and a smile on her face.

"I didn't even think you liked me," I say to her reflection. "Sometimes you're so—"

"Bitchy? Yeah, I know. It's a defense mechanism. And I was trying to distance myself from you."

"Because of... this?" I turn and wrap my arms around her waist.

"Yes. I wasn't sure if my attention would be welcomed," she replies.

"Even after we kissed at the bar?"

"Even after that. We were both drunk. Things happen. I was just trying to protect myself. And you. But right now, we better get you downstairs." She kisses my temple and lets go of me.

"Maybe it's better if we go down separately," I suggest. "I mean, I know we're swapping, but I don't know if you want the others to know about... this."

She considers that for a moment. "You're right, I don't want them to know. Not right now, anyway. You go ahead. I'll clean myself up and be down shortly." She smiles and reaches for a towel.

My legs wobble as I make my way down the stairs. It's been a long time since they've done that. The sex with Andrew has been great recently, but not like that. Tomorrow, when this pill has worked its way out of my system, when I'm back in my own home with my kids and Dawn's children are back from her sister's, all of this will hit me. And I'll have to figure out what it means. But I'm not ready to face it yet.

Downstairs, Amy and Miles are on the sofa. Her white dress has been discarded, and Miles's pants are puddled around his ankles as he thrusts roughly into her. Lewis sits on the far side of the sofa, watching, his eyes glassy and his hand in his pants.

I walk past without saying anything. It's surreal. *If anyone heard about what we do out here on Madison Lane...* I almost laugh.

I find Andrew at the kitchen table with a glass of whiskey in his hand. He's dressed, but his clothes are wrinkled, his hair disheveled. He looks up at me when I enter, but his expression is inscrutable. Hard, almost.

"You okay?" I walk over and put a hand on his shoulder.

He shrugs it off and tosses back the rest of his whiskey.

Well, that was easier to read. Andrew is clearly mad at me about something.

"Pass me that bottle." He points to the counter.

"You sure you should?" I ask, already moving toward the bottle.

He pours a generous serving and downs half of it in one gulp. Soft cries of pleasure emanate from the living room, and Andrew's lips tighten before he finishes his glass.

"Come on," he says irritably, "let's get home." He clunks his glass onto the table, stands, and grabs my hand. "We'll go out the back. No reason to draw attention to ourselves. I'm pretty sure the rest of the neighborhood gossips about us already."

He tugs my hand, and we exit through the back door, following a walkway around the corner of the house to the street. Andrew looks back at the house, his face rigid under the hazy streetlights. He grabs my hand and drags me down the block, like Dawn and Lewis's house is the last place he wants to be.

Maybe he's the one who can't cope with this after practically begging me to do it. I glance back at the house one more time and see Dawn standing in her bedroom window, watching us leave.

18

Andrew walks so fast I can barely keep up with him. I stop and quickly pull off my heels before running down the block to catch him. The concrete is rough on my feet, so I rise onto my toes.

"Hey, hey, what's going on?" I tug on his arm to slow him down. "Was tonight a 'rainstorm' moment?"

"Rainsto—oh, you mean that stupid safe word. No, it wasn't a rainstorm moment. I'm fine with what happened tonight except—" He stops. "Miles."

"What did Miles do?" I ask, confused. "The last time I saw him, he and Amy were, you know, otherwise engaged."

"Exactly."

I pause, waiting for an explanation. Miles wasn't the name I thought he'd blurt. If anything, I thought Lewis and I might have triggered Andrew's foul mood.

"Why'd he have to go and sleep with Amy after I did?" Andrew says in a peevish tone.

"Why do you care?" I stop walking and force Andrew to face me. I'm shocked. Andrew has a moody side. I've always known that. But he has a stressful job where people complain to him all day. I usually give him a pass. But tonight, he sounds like a spoiled brat. "Is there some reason it's such a big deal to you? He's her husband."

"That's my point. It was supposed to be a swap," he snaps. "I'm just saying that it seems to go against the rules."

I shake my head and start walking again, eager to get our conversation off the street. "You didn't care this much about the rules that first night when you slept with Amy."

But he isn't listening. "Maybe next time I should suggest that we have a one-partner rule." Andrew digs into his pocket and pulls out the keys to the front door. "Otherwise, it's just weird."

"You're being ridiculous," I snap, annoyed at his suggestion. And not just because Amy wasn't the only one to have two partners tonight. "Sounds to me like you're jealous more than anything."

"I'm not jealous. I just think Miles took advantage of the arrangement to sleep with two women tonight."

"Is something going on with you two? With you and Amy?" I stop on the edge of the sidewalk.

Andrew's face is orange in the cast of the streetlights. He lets out a short, sharp laugh before shaking his head. "You're crazy. Why would something be going on when we're literally swapping wives at parties? Like, what would be the benefit?"

"I'm not crazy. Come on, Andrew. You aren't mad about me and Lewis, but Miles being with Amy makes you angry? I know what this is." I yank away from him and stalk down the block then turn back to him. "You know what? Rainstorm!"

Andrew runs to catch up with me. "What the hell is that supposed to mean?"

"We're done. You said so yourself. Safe word and we're out. This isn't how it's supposed to be, Andrew. This is supposed to be something fun and exciting. You're not supposed to have feelings for the other people. So we're stopping," I practically scream at him in the middle of the road. "It's over!"

Andrew's eyes widen with shock. He dashes toward me and knocks me to the ground. I didn't even hear the SUV, but I see it as it runs up onto the sidewalk where we were just standing. The oversized tires leave deep indentations in the otherwise neat grass borders. The engine revs loudly, and the SUV pulls away with a squeal. I'm on my hands and knees, pavement digging into my flesh, and Andrew bends over me.

"Holy shit. Petra, are you okay?"

He helps me to my feet, and I flinch when I straighten my legs, my knees skinned and bloody. He runs his hands over my arms and back, checking for injuries.

"I'm fine," I mumble, my heart racing.

Someone tried to kill us. *What the hell?*

I watch as the taillights disappear into the night. "I don't suppose you managed to see anything, did you? License plate number or a person?"

"No. It was too fast. It just... happened. I'm sorry I tossed you to the ground, but—"

"A couple of skinned knees seem like a fair trade for my life." I place my hand over my pounding heart. "I might die of a heart attack, though."

"Come on, let's get inside before they come back."

He grabs my hand, and I wince, realizing my palms still sting from where they slapped the asphalt, but I don't pull away as he leads me quickly up our walkway and into the house. I tremble as the babysitter hurries into the kitchen.

"I saw through the window," she says. "Are you okay?"

I open a cupboard to grab a glass, but my hands are shaking. Andrew is busy locking the door, so Kaitlyn pours me a whiskey.

"Did you see the plate number?" I ask.

Kaitlyn shakes her head. "No, sorry. It was just a blur of lights."

"Are the kids okay?" I ask.

She nods. "Fast asleep."

"How are you getting home?" Andrew asks.

"I planned to walk," she says.

He shakes his head. "I'll give you a lift after I clean Petra up." He turns to me. "Will you be okay on your own for ten minutes?"

My heart pounds, and I'm not sure I will be, but I also don't want Kaitlyn walking home alone after what just happened. "Yeah. Of course."

He runs the taps and dampens a cloth as I sit at the dining room table. Kaitlyn heads into the house to get her jacket and purse.

"Andrew, what's going on around here?" I wince as he smears a biting antibacterial cream on my scraped hands.

"I don't know, honey. I don't know." He bends over to patch up my knees, and I wonder if this has anything to do with our little swapping game and if we've gone too far.

19

"Who?" I prop my phone between my chin and shoulder and heft a couple of bags from the trunk of my rental car.

The small four-door was the only vehicle available when we rented one to replace my stolen SUV, and its tiny size takes some getting used to. Andrew refuses to drive it, preferring his shiny Audi instead.

"Oh, from the police station. Sure, hang on." I shift the bags around and get a better hold on the phone that threatens to slip from its precarious perch. "Yeah, I can come in. Now?" I check my watch to see how long I have before the kids finish school. "Sure, give me half an hour. I'll be there." I end the call and drag my bags into the house.

Less than forty-five minutes go by when I pull my rental into the lot of the local police station. It sits in what would be our downtown area if the suburbs had downtowns. It's a small building that, from the front, looks like it should be a chic boutique or maybe a hip brewery. I park and make my way inside, surprised to see that hardwood floors and plantation shutters decorate the lobby. A few well-placed plants give the place a tropical bungalow feel.

I introduce myself to the officer manning the reception desk, and soon, I'm led into the back. The young officer sets me up in an office off the hallway and assures me someone will be with me soon.

That someone is a middle-aged woman with a brunette bob and broad shoulders. She greets me with a handshake and introduces herself as Detective Sandra Buchanan. Then she settles into the chair on the opposite side of the desk and flips open a folder.

"Okay, you had the white Escalade—nice car by the way." She glances up from the report. "Unfortunately, it was found burned out near the dump way out past Highway 78."

"Near the dump?" I question, confused. "Why would it be out there?"

"Can I get you to fill out this statement?" She doesn't answer my question but passes me a clipboard and a pen. "You'll need the report for your insurance."

"Sure." I glance down at the paper. "Why would someone do that to my car?"

"Truthfully, it was probably just a bunch of joyriders. Bored kids most likely." She taps the clipboard. "Make sure you include everything you remember."

"Right." I uncap the pen. "Wait, you think a couple of kids stole a ninety-thousand-dollar car, took it for a spin, then set fire to it? You don't think that burning out someone's car is kind of... sinister?"

"Should I think it's sinister for a reason?" She eyes me now, her attention piqued. "Joyriding happens all the time, and kids burn the cars to get rid of evidence." She shrugs. "But why does it seem sinister to you? Is something else going on?"

"Actually, yes. I was followed by a black SUV the day my car was stolen," I say.

"Okay," she says.

"And my car was scratched that morning. Then, a couple of nights ago, another black SUV—or the same one, I don't know—came right at me and my husband on the street. It almost mowed us down. Then there was the pile of dung in the road—"

"Hold on a moment, Mrs. Ross." The detective leans back in her chair as if floored by my words. "I'm not sure which thread to pull at first here. Let's start with the car that almost mowed down you and your husband. What happened there?"

"A couple of days ago, my husband and I were walking home from a friend's house." I stop and clear my throat. "We'd had a game night." *Shut up, shut up,* I tell myself. *She doesn't need all this information.* "Anyhow, we think a black SUV tried to run us over. Or lost control, I don't know."

The detective spears me with a look. "Go on."

"I mean, it could have just... jumped the curb, I guess? But it seemed deliberate. And it recovered well afterwards. Whoever was driving carried on like nothing had happened. That seemed suspicious to me. Most people would get out and make sure we were okay." I clutch my hands in my lap.

"Why didn't you call us right away?"

"I—we, didn't really think about it. It happened so fast, we weren't sure it was deliberate," I confess. "I guess we should have called. With neither of us hurt we just wanted to go to bed."

"Yes, you should have called." The detective gives me a smile that's not particularly friendly. "Now, what's this about dung?"

"We did call about that."

"Oh, on Madison Lane?"

I nod.

"I do remember that." She lets out a low chuckle. "It's not every day you have officers investigating a pile of dung left in the street. At the time, we figured it was fly-tipping, but with the other incidents you've told me about, it does seem suspicious."

"Right!" I say, excited she's taking me seriously.

"For now, what I want you to do is fill out that statement. I'll get you a report for your insurance company. From now on, keep a log if anything like that happens again." She closes the folder and slides it into a filing cabinet "And maybe consider calling us next time someone tries to kill you. It's in our job description."

"Thanks for coming." Dawn halfway stands as I approach the table.

For a second, I think she'll lean over and kiss me, but she just pats my arm and sits back down. She pushes out a chair with her foot, and I sit. The small café isn't crowded at this time of the morning. And it's not Marco's this time. Dawn wanted to meet somewhere away from her colleagues.

"Shouldn't you be at the school?" I ask Dawn as I study one of the small, printed menus stacked on the end of the table.

"I've swapped with a teacher friend until lunch. I thought we needed to get together in a neutral place, just us girls, and kind of hash out the other night." Dawn flips over a menu. "Also, this place has excellent pie."

"We're waiting for Amy?" I look around.

Except for an elderly man in a booth at the far end, we're

the only people in the café. A bored-looking server lounges at the counter, thumbing through her phone.

"Aren't we always?" Dawn snorts.

Just then, Amy bustles through the door, Hunter on her hip. "Sorry, sorry, emergency diaper change." Without asking, she deposits Hunter onto my lap and walks away. She comes back dragging a portable high chair. "Sorry, sorry," she repeats, plucking the baby off my lap. She fastens him into the chair and dumps a pile of cereal O's in front of him. "So, how's it going?"

I look at Amy in her pink sweater set and realize I don't really want to talk to her. I'd prefer if it were just Dawn and me at this meeting. But I still smile a hello as she settles in at the table.

Then I turn to Dawn. "They found my car."

"Really? Are you getting it back?" She raises a hand and waves over the server. "I'm so glad they found it."

"Yeah, well, it was destroyed," I reply. "Burned out is what the officer told me. And that's not all. Listen to this." I tell them about the SUV following me and trying to run over Andrew and me.

"Oh my goodness," Amy says. "Is Andrew okay?"

Her concern for my husband rankles me. Invisible hackles stand up on the back of my neck. "He's fine."

"Petra, that's some serious shit," Dawn says. "You guys could have been badly hurt or killed. It sounds like you have a stalker."

"I know. And I've racked my brain trying to figure out why. Why would someone target me? I haven't done anything wrong. Have I?" I glance back and forth between Dawn and Amy.

Amy just drops her head and looks away.

"You're one of the nicest people I know. No one should have a reason to come after you." Dawn pats my hand.

"The only thing I can think of is"—I lower my voice—"our game nights."

"What would make you say that?" Amy says. "We all participated, so why would you be the only one getting harassed?" She mixes a sippy cup of juice for a fussy Hunter and passes it to him. "Nothing has happened to us."

"Not yet, anyway." The words sound more ominous than I intended.

Amy bristles, sitting taller in her seat. "That almost sounded like a threat."

"Oh, for fuck's sake, Amy. Do you think I'm threatening you? I'm the one who was almost run over!" I snap.

Dawn's expression changes. Her eyes narrow slightly, as though she's trying to suss me out. I know I'm not exactly myself today. A hot temper brews beneath my skin.

Amy redirects her attention to a fussy Hunter as Dawn's eyes flick back and forth between us.

"I don't know what's going on with you two," Dawn says. "But I'd like to discuss the other night."

"What about it?" Amy asks.

"Well, Lewis is hinting that we should do it again."

"I don't know," I say slowly. "Don't you think maybe we should take a breather? Some time to process everything that's happened?" I glance sideways at Amy and notice that she's watching me.

"Miles has been saying he's ready," Amy says.

"Shocker, the guys are ready for a repeat." I roll my eyes. "But I'm not sure I am. What about you two?"

"I mean, if Miles is ready, I guess I could be, too." Amy fidgets with one of Hunter's stuffed animals. Her eyes flick to me. "What about Andrew?"

"Are you asking specifically about Andrew for a reason? Why not Lewis?" I ask.

"Enough," Dawn says sharply. "This is exactly what I was afraid would happen. I'll tell Lewis we need more time before we have another 'game night.' I think we all need to go home and think about what we really want out of this." She stands and drops her napkin on the table. "Amy, I'll talk to you later."

I stand. "I'll walk you out." With a glance over my shoulder at Amy, I trail Dawn to the front of the café.

"Listen." She turns to me. "It's easy for someone like Amy to catch feelings. You have to cut her some slack."

"But she's caught feelings for *my* husband," I say. "What if it were Lewis?"

I hold back on the part that's really bothering me. The part where I'm pretty sure Andrew feels something for Amy.

"I'd be thrilled. Might give me some free time." She smiles. It could be my imagination, but her smile seems tinged with sadness. Perhaps because we haven't had a chance to talk about what *we* did at the last game night. "Look, I'll talk to you soon. Try not to dwell on this stuff with Amy. I don't think she knows what she's putting you through." I'm surprised when she leans in and gives me a hug. Then she slips something into my hand.

I head back to the table to say goodbye to Amy. "Sorry for snapping." I give her a quick hug.

I'm surprised she doesn't return the apology. In fact, I'm annoyed. But I take some of Dawn's advice and don't dwell on it. Back in my car, I unfold the small piece of paper Dawn slipped into my hand. There, in neat script, is a date, time, and address. I google the address, and my pulse quickens. Dawn has given me the address to a hotel. She wants to meet me alone.

20

"Call the babysitter if you have to," I tell Andrew. I lean forward, inches from the bathroom mirror as I swipe mascara along my lashes.

"You're getting awfully dressed up just to meet with an old college friend." Andrew leans against the doorframe, his arms crossed, the top button of his shirt unbuttoned and his tie hanging free. "I have things to do this evening, too, you know."

"I may not get to see Sarah again for ages." The lie burns in my throat. "We roomed together for years."

"I remember her. Total nerd. You sure a night out with her warrants that kind of dress?" He gestures to my short black skirt.

"I want to look nice." I shrug, dab perfume behind my ears, and check my lipstick. "I haven't been out in so long. Well, unless you count those game nights. If you have work to do, just give the kids their iPads. I'll allow it for the night."

"Wow, this must be really important to you if you're allowing unfettered iPad access." He laughs. "Okay, fine. But the sitter's number is on the fridge, right?"

"Right." I slip on my heels and study myself in the mirror. "Don't wait up." I walk out of the room, down the stairs, and outside to my car.

I take the train into the city then grab an Uber to the hotel. By the time I arrive, I'm so nervous, I'm practically shaking. I stand in front of the glittering building, looking up at the endless expanse of windows above me. I'm there so long that a doorman walks over and asks if I need anything.

"Oh, just meeting someone." My face flushes at the thought that he knows exactly why I'm here. I follow him to the door and step inside the lobby.

Giving myself a couple of minutes to calm down, I study the lobby's marble floors and crystal chandeliers. The whole place gives off an air of luxuriousness and money. Finally, I pull out my phone and call Dawn.

"I'm here," I say, my voice higher than usual.

"Great," she says. "See you soon."

A few minutes pass while I pace the lobby floor, my heels clicking sharply on the marble. Finally, the elevator doors open, and Dawn steps out. She's a vision in a shimmering gold wrap dress and red-bottomed shoes.

"Hi." She gives me a quick hug. "You look fantastic." Her eyes travel over me and my tight dress.

I may as well be standing in the lobby naked.

"Come on. I've got a suite." She grabs my hand and leads me into the elevator, pushing the button to the forty-seventh floor.

When the doors close, she grabs my shoulders and pushes me against the elevator wall. Her tongue swipes at my lips, and I open them, letting her explore me until the elevator pings and the door slides open.

Our shoes are silent on the lush carpet. The sudden hush means I hear my heart beating hard against my ribs. We stop at door 4712, and she taps a keycard on the sensor. The lock clicks, and Dawn pushes open the door.

Then the smile fades from my lips. Lewis lounges on the small sofa in the sitting area.

"What is this?" I stop in the entrance, turning to Dawn.

"It's a party, baby," Lewis says with a calculated grin.

"Dawn?" I can't keep the betrayal from my voice. I can't believe she'd spring this on me.

"Sorry, I thought if I told you, you wouldn't come." She reaches for me, but I pull away.

"You're right, I wouldn't have."

"Hey, don't be that way." Lewis stands and makes his way over to the wet bar. "Let's have a drink."

"What about the rules?" I ask.

"We don't have any rules here." He pours a healthy glug of bourbon into a glass then casually walks over to me.

I can't deny he's a handsome man. Tall, broad shouldered, well groomed. During our last two encounters, I felt pleasure at his hands on my body. But it's Dawn I wanted to be with, not him.

"I thought we weren't allowed to meet individually. No meeting each other outside of the group."

"Hey, we're half the group." Lewis smiles. "Nothing individual about it."

I hand him back the glass of bourbon.

He shrugs and takes a gulp. "Besides, weren't you meeting my wife here? Alone?" He draws out the last word and raises his eyebrows.

"Dawn?" I turn to her.

"Lewis wants to watch. Us." She casts me a sheepish glance.

"You told him about us?" I'm shocked. I thought it was something we were keeping to ourselves.

"Yeah, she did," Lewis interjects. "And I definitely want to be in on it next time."

Dawn reaches for my hand and pulls me to her. "It's okay. He just wants to watch. He was very excited, you know, thinking about me and you together that night." Her fingertips brush the back of my hand. "It could be fun." She leans forward and kisses me, slowly and softly.

When she pulls away, Lewis watches us, bourbon glass held close to his mouth, his thumb tracing his bottom lip. My eyes flash down to the bulging front of his slacks.

He notices me looking and grabs himself. "You like that?"

"Come on." Dawn turns me and urges me toward the suite's bedroom. I let her, a delicious tension building in my stomach. I want to be with Dawn again, and if Lewis wants to watch, let him.

"Just watching," I say. "Those are my rules."

Dawn takes me to the bed while Lewis drapes himself over a club chair positioned in the corner. His glass of bourbon dangles from his fingers, and his eyelids are heavy from liquor and lust.

Dawn strips my clothes away and lowers me to the bed. We twine around each other, tasting and touching soft skin. Dawn's skin is pliant under my lips. She doesn't protest when I roll her underneath me and let my hands roam across her body, taking in the curve of her waist and the jut of her hip bones. I lower myself between her thighs, lost in her low cries.

A hand around my waist pulls me away from Dawn. Lewis stands behind me, pressing his hips into me.

"You're just supposed to watch." I push at him.

"You're so fucking hot. Both of you. I need to touch you," he murmurs.

I glance at Dawn, and she nods yes. Lewis's eyes light up.

He pushes me onto my knees, and enters me from behind. His fingers dig into my waist, and his movements are hard, full of fury.

"Lewis, you're hurting me." I try to inch away.

"Stop, Lewis." Dawn shoves at his shoulders.

He laughs and rams against my hips. I kick my heel back and make contact with something fleshy. Whatever it is makes Lewis grunt and drop his hands. I scuttle across the bed and jump off the other side.

"Bastard," I spit at him as I snatch my clothes off the floor. "You really can't follow rules, can you?" I pull on my clothes, grab my shoes, and turn to Dawn. "Sorry, Dawn."

I run to the door and just before I slip out, Lewis rounds on Dawn. Instead of turning around, I run to the elevator and punch the button, willing the doors to open.

As the elevator takes me down, I debate going back to the room. Lewis seems out of control. He didn't care about breaking the rules that he established for swapping partners, and he didn't seem to care about ignoring boundaries we set for him.

I lean against the mirror, hoping she's okay. Then I straighten my clothes and hair and make a beeline for the lounge when the elevator doors open onto the lobby. From there, I call Dawn. If she doesn't answer, I'll call the police.

21

I feel a hand on my back and turn to find Dawn standing behind me. I sit at the bar, a glass of white wine in front of me. Dawn's eyes are red, and I motion for the bartender to bring another glass. Dawn slips onto the stool beside me and takes the glass gratefully.

"I didn't think you'd stay." She takes a sip of her wine.

"I wanted to make sure you were okay." I pick up a napkin off the bar and shred it.

"Lewis says he's sorry, by the way. He just got carried away. He wants you to know he's not an asshole." Dawn watches as I destroy another napkin.

"I think his actions speak louder than his words." I sigh and dump the pile of napkin pieces onto the bar. "What can we do?"

"About what?"

"About what we're doing." I glance around at the other patrons and lean toward Dawn. "About the swapping. We can't keep doing this."

"I know." Dawn sighs, wiping her face wearily with her

hands. "I thought it was kind of fun at first, but now..." Her voice trails off, and she stares over the bar.

"This is getting insane. We never should have done this, Dawn. You know that. We have to stop. All of it, the game nights, meetups like this. This is fucking with our heads. And our marriages. I should go." I spin on my stool and reach for my purse.

"Wait." Dawn places a hand on my arm.

When I turn to her, tears drip slowly down her face.

"We can still be friends," I assure her. "Coffee dates and cookouts. But everything else has to stop. We have to get our marriages back on track." I'm not sure I even believe what I'm saying. *Can a marriage go back to normal after what we've done? What I've done?*

"I don't think I can." Dawn sniffles and rubs her fingers under her eyes, checking for running mascara. "The thing is, I don't want to be married anymore. Not to Lewis, anyhow."

"Not you and Miles," I say. "Tell me you aren't."

"No. Not Miles. You, Petra. I want you."

She says it so softly I have to lean in to hear her. I don't know what to do, so I put my arm around her shoulders and pull her to me. She cries quietly against my shoulder. I run my hand up and down her back.

"It'll be okay. We'll figure this out." I grab the napkin under my drink and hand it to her so she can dab at her eyes.

"I didn't scare you off?" She hiccups.

"No, you didn't. I... like you, too."

"But not the same way I like you." Her voice sounds small and childlike, totally unlike the take-charge Dawn I'm used to.

Her vulnerability shocks me. Her admission is far more intimate than sleeping with her.

"I... don't know how to answer that. I think you know I'm

attracted to you. And I care for you. I don't want you hurt. But I still love my husband."

"I understand." Dawn nods slowly. "Let's keep this between us, huh?"

"Absolutely." I mime locking my lips with a key. "And we agreed, no more swapping?"

"No more swapping. I'll talk to Amy. I know she's not, uh, your favorite person right now." Dawn grabs her glass of wine, downing it in one swallow.

"Thanks. I'll have to hash it out with her eventually. I'm just not ready to right now. I think it'll take a little more time before I can handle her gently. You okay?" I rub Dawn's arm.

"I am. I wonder what the guys will say when we tell them the games are over." Dawn puts her glass on the bar and raises a finger to get the bartender's attention. "One more."

"I bet they won't be happy. But we have to stop before this all implodes. I don't even want to think about what the fallout would be like."

"You're right. Listen, I better get back up to Lewis. You'll be okay getting home alone?"

"I'll be fine. Yeah, you better get upstairs."

She leans forward and kisses my cheek. "We'll talk soon, okay?"

"Sure." I smile. Then I gather my coat and bag and walk out of the bar.

The train ride home gives me too much time to think. I mull over everything that's happened during the past few weeks, trying to pinpoint where everything went wrong. I want to lay the blame on Miles for providing the drugs or Lewis for pushing for another game night. But I know we're all to blame. We were all bored. We were looking for excitement, something to take us out of our suburban lives for a while. I'm just as much to blame as the rest of them. I didn't say no. I didn't back out. I went along with everything. Even tonight, I wanted to see Dawn so much that I came out alone, after everything that's happened with the stalker. *What if someone followed me? What if someone tried to kill me?* That's how addictive this has become.

By the time the train reaches the station, I don't have answers, but I know we made the right decision to stop the games.

I walk off the platform and out into the cold night, where my car waits on the far side of the commuter lot. It strikes me that I lied to Andrew about going out with an old friend tonight, and now I have to lie to him about why I'm home early. I'm sure I'll figure something out by the time I reach home.

I open my car door, still the rental, and toss my bag onto the passenger seat before sliding into my seat and clicking my seat belt. I lock the doors before quickly checking my phone. Nothing, no texts from anyone, which at this point, I'll take as a good sign. It's only when I look up from my phone that I notice the truck on the far side of the lot. Its lights are on, pointed at me.

Fuck.

My heart slams into my throat. I start the car, my eyes still on the truck. *It's not an SUV, but what if this creep has two vehicles?* The truck stays where it is, unmoving, but I sense the person in the driver's seat watching me. And waiting.

I speed from the lot, hitting the curb on the way out. When I check the mirror to see if the truck is following me, nothing's there. But that doesn't slow my beating heart. Or stop the dread building in my stomach.

22

Children stream around me, searching for their moms and dads, chattering about their day to friends, displaying that just-out-of-school joy that only children have. I stand in the clutch of parents at the gates, waiting for Olivia and Luca. Finally, I see the red knit cap Luca wore to school this morning bobbing among the crowd of kids. Olivia walks beside him, her hand firmly clasped around his.

"Mommy, Mommy!" Luca spots me and pulls away, dashing closer while Olivia trails behind him, calling his name. He slams into my knees and hugs them then immediately tells me about the "lizard man" who visited school that day. "So cool, he had dragons!"

"He had chameleons." Olivia snorts. "And an iguana. One was called Tommy. He was huge."

"Yeah, as huge as a dragon!" Luca skips around me, chanting "dragons, dragons" while Olivia rolls her eyes.

"Okay, you two. Let's get to the car. You can tell me about the dragons then." I pluck Luca's lunchbox from his fingers and take his hand.

Olivia clutches the hem of my jacket. Just as we're about

to cross the street, I see Dawn and Amy standing near the gate.

I stop for a second, unsure if they've seen me. I haven't spoken to either of them since the night with Dawn at the hotel. I meant it when I said I was through with the whole thing. Whether or not I can be friends with them again remains to be seen. Until I figure it out, though, I'll keep my distance. Dawn glances up, sees me, and some unnamed emotion flashes across her face. Amy follows her gaze, and her expression freezes when she spots me. No need to wonder what Amy thinks of me these days. All I do is wave, take my children by the hands, and walk across the road to my car.

The afternoon passes in a haze of snacks and a game of hide-and-seek. After I've pulled Luca out of the linen closet for the third time—it's the only place he ever hides—I park the kids in front of the TV, put on cartoons, and start dinner. Mac and cheese tonight, though in our house, whether mac and cheese is considered a meal or a side dish is a big debate. I'm in the side dish camp.

I just put the pasta water on to boil and am shredding cheese when the lights flicker. I stop and look up at the overhead fixture. *Is the bulb about to burn out?* Before I can decide, all the lights go out, and I hear screams from the family room.

"Hang on. I'm coming. Please stop screaming!" I yell at the kids.

I dig into my pocket and pull out my phone, tabbing on the flashlight function. Then I dig into the junk drawer and come up with a couple of small flashlights. I quickly make sure they work before heading into the family room.

"Okay, here's what's going to happen." I hand the kids the

flashlights. "You stay here with your lights, and Mommy will go to the basement to see if the breaker flipped. Here, play a game." I grab the iPad and open a game for them. "I won't be long, and I'll be able to hear you if you yell, okay? Just stay right here." I give them each a quick rub on the head and go back into the kitchen.

Before heading into the basement, I try calling Andrew but get no answer, as usual. He's becoming harder and harder to reach these days. My eyes trail to the far side of the room, landing on the door that leads to the basement.

I hate the basement.

Pulling it open, I peer down the stairs into the darkness. My phone only illuminates the first few steps. Everything that falls beyond the light is pitch black. I shudder. I was so glad when we bought a house with a laundry room located upstairs. Still, I'm a grown-ass woman, and I can check a goddamn fuse box.

An unwanted thought pops into my mind. *What if it's the stalker? What if he's down here waiting?* And then I dismiss it. I'd know, wouldn't I? If someone had broken into the house.

I put my hand on the rail and carefully make my way down, my foot searching out each step slowly and deliberately. When I reach the bottom, I sweep my light around quickly. All I see are stacks of holiday decorations and an old exercise bike. The power box is on the far side, so as fast as possible, I make my way across the dusty floor and pull open the cover. It looks like one of the fuses is gone. Nothing seems faulty. It's more like someone has *removed* the fuse. I scan the ground around my feet and see it near the wall. *Could it have dropped out on its own?*

Something crunches behind me—a boot on dusty ground. I turn sharply, sweeping the area with my phone's light. But I can't see beyond what the beam touches. Those shadows lie rich with possibilities and hidden potential. Anything, or anyone, could be hiding there. The back of my neck prickles with tension.

I'm being watched. I know it in the marrow of my bones. I know it like I know the sky is blue. Quickly, I bend and snatch the fuse from the floor, then try to shove it into its spot. I need light. I need to see where I can move safely.

The blow comes out of nowhere, right between my shoulder blades. Pain radiates up and across my back, numbing my arm. It almost takes me to my knees, but I catch myself on the wall. The fuse slips between my finger and skitters across the floor. Spinning, I swing my phone wildly, searching for the intruder. The light bounces across the space, flashing like a disco ball. I hear the swish of the hammer coming down before it flies out of the dark. I raise my arms and duck, one thought pounding through my brain. I'm going to die.

23

When the hammer strikes, catching my elbow, pain shoots up my arm. I cry out, grabbing my hurt arm as I move, trying to get away from the attacker. *But where are they?*

The air changes almost imperceptibly around me. I sense the hammer raising for a second attack. I duck. The heavy object collides with the wall behind my head. But from that movement, I know vaguely that the person is right in front of me.

I lower my head and ram as hard as can into the body standing before me. They "umph" as I connect with their chest, then they tumble backward and hit the floor. An opportunity. A small one, but I need to make the most of it. I stumble as I rush toward the staircase. I have no time to use my phone as a light. Instead, I rely on my instincts. It's dark, but I know this house. I'm a few steps away from the intruder when they grab my ankle. I kick out, and my foot connects with something, possibly a face. I'm not sure. Whatever I did hurt them. They grunt and let me go.

The bottom step trips me up, and I almost land on my

face, but adrenaline keeps me going. I need to get the kids out of this house. Using my good arm, I clamber up the steep steps, practically on all fours. I don't look back, but I can hear them a few steps behind me. I climb faster and finally burst out of the basement door into the kitchen.

It's not as dark here, and my eyes immediately pick out shapes that could trip me.

"Olivia! Luca!"

The hall between the kitchen and family room seems immeasurably long, especially with the pain spiraling across my back and up my neck. I half stumble, half run toward my children, yelling at them to hide.

The blow to my head catches me off guard, and I pitch forward, my face squarely hitting the carpet. *Did they hear me? Did they hide?* It's all I can think about with the pain radiating through my body. I force myself to roll over and face my attacker. But I don't recognize anything. The intruder stands over me, dressed in black from head to toe. A ski mask covers their features. The kids scream somewhere in the house. *God, don't let them witness this. Don't let them see their mom be murdered.* The figure standing over me raises the hammer, ready to put me out of my misery once and for all.

"Run!" I yell.

The figure hesitates for a second, hammer still raised. *What are they waiting for?* I can't do anything. I'm helpless. Then they walk away. My heart sinks. They're headed toward the living room. Toward the children.

No.

I scramble to my knees and fling myself at the shadowy figure. My fingers brush their jacket. I grab a handful of the fabric and pull as hard as I can. The kids stand in the living room doorway, holding on to each other, the iPad discarded on the floor. The flickering light from the game illuminates their terrified faces as they watch me tussle with a violent attacker. They must be too scared to hide. Too frightened to leave me.

We fall to the floor, and the hammer tumbles onto the floorboards. My fingers brush the handle before the assailant snatches it away from me. They spin back toward my children, hammer raised. Without thinking, I throw myself between them.

"Run!" I yell.

This time, the kids move.

Olivia grabs Luca by the shirt and hauls him through to the kitchen. *Hide inside the pantry,* I think. She's a clever girl. She'll know what to do. I pray it's enough, but I know I have to keep this person busy. Though blood spills from the wound on my head, my arm might be broken, and my back is killing me, I lunge for them one more time.

This time, the hammer hits my shoulder. I stumble back, off balance. Just before I hit the floor, bright lights flash across the family room. The kids scream again. I hear running footsteps.

Please don't hurt my children, I think as the world goes black.

24

"Oh my god, Petra! Petra!"

Andrew, I realize.

"Olivia, call 911, just like we practiced, okay, honey?" he says. His voice sounds panicked.

The kids sob softly, but Olivia says, "Yes, Daddy."

"Petra, please."

Andrew tries to help me sit up, but I can't. It hurts too much. I know if I sit up, I'll puke. But I can't find the strength to push him away.

A low, sorrowful groan escapes my lips, and Andrew gently places me back on the floor. It's like he just realized he most likely was making everything worse. My thoughts are strange and fuzzy. I keep thinking about the intruder but also stupid things like how we need milk and why Andrew couldn't be a psychiatrist rather than a therapist. That way he would have a medical degree and would know not to move someone with a head injury.

I can just make out Olivia's small voice, high-pitched and frightened, as she uses her dad's phone to call 911. She sounds so much younger than six as she recites our address.

Absurdly, a memory of us teaching the kids our new address surfaces. *1417 Madison Lane.* It took Luca a while longer to memorize the numbers. Olivia got it right away. My smart girl and my beautiful boy. Their faces appear in my mind as the world blackens again.

The acrid smell of alcohol invades my senses. Crisp sheets crinkle beneath me. Then the pain comes flooding in. It's everywhere, but it isn't as bad as I remembered, and the surface beneath me is comfortable. Before I open my eyes, I know I'm in the hospital, no longer half-conscious in our hallway.

"I think she's waking," Andrew says.

Shoes squeak softly on a tiled floor. Finally, my eyelids flutter open, and the light blinds me. I blink rapidly until the person in front of me comes into focus.

"There we are. Petra, I'm Dr. Vogel. How are you feeling?" The man standing above me wears a white coat with a stethoscope hanging out of the pocket. A name tag pinned to his jacket is still too blurry to read.

"Um, okay," I mumble. I'm lying. The pounding in my head is so fierce, I can hardly hear.

"I'll be the judge of that," he says.

He checks my vitals, starting with my blood pressure, then he uses a thin penlight to check my pupils. Finally, he grabs a chart from the end of the bed and makes a few notes.

"Let me tell you what's going on. Your spine and elbow are badly bruised, and you have a concussion. The good news is nothing is broken. You'll be out of commission for a couple of weeks, but you'll be just fine. If you take it easy, that is."

"My kids," I croak, my throat dry.

The doctor notices and hands me a cup of water from the bedside table.

"The kids are fine, honey." Andrew comes into view. "They're at my mom's. They'll be fine." He pats my hand gently. "Do you need more water?"

I pass him the cup.

"I'll have the nurse bring you something for the pain." The doctor snaps my chart shut.

Andrew brings me another cup of water with ice chips. I take small sips until my throat stops burning.

"Knock, knock," the nurse says as she pushes open the door. "Two things really quick. I'll run an IV line if that's okay. The pain meds act quicker that way. Also, a police officer is here to see you. If you're up to speak with her."

"Yeah, sure. To both," I say.

I try to shift into a sitting position, but the nurse shoos my arms away and uses a remote to raise the head of the bed. She's swift and efficient with the IV line, and by the time the police officer knocks on the door, the pain in my head and back melts away, replaced by a mellow warmth.

I recognize the detective right away. Buchanan, the woman I spoke to at the precinct about my car. She's in a gray suit today. It has a stain on the lapel.

"You feel like talking?" she asks.

"Sure." The pain medication slurs my reply.

The detective settles into the chair beside my bed and pulls out a notebook. "Are you in a lot of pain?"

"Oh, just a tad," I say.

She lifts her eyebrows. "You've had a tough go of it. I think we can safely say that stalker exists now. And they are highly dangerous." Her eyes lower to her notebook as she reads something back. "Okay, we've already taken your husband's statement. And we'll get one from the children if you and your husband agree. We have wonderful social workers on call who can help, and of course, you or your husband will be with them."

"Okay." My eyes flick to Andrew, and he nods.

"Good. Now, tell me what you remember about yesterday." Her pen remains poised over the notebook.

"Yesterday? I've been out for a day?"

"Yes, you have. Your body needed the rest." Andrew stands by the bed again, holding my hand.

I turn to the detective, and she nods, encouraging me to talk. I tell her about the lights going out, finding the fuse on the floor, and the intruder in the basement. Andrew adds something about finding one of the small basement windows unlocked. Detective Buchanan nods as she writes everything down, occasionally stopping me to ask a question or have me clarify something I said.

"Are you sure that's everything?" the detective asks. When I nod yes, she flips her notebook closed. She pulls out a business card and lays it on the table beside me. "If you remember anything else, even if you don't think it's important, call me." She says goodbye and heads for the door.

It's only as I watch the detective walk away and her suit jacket hitches up at her waist that I remember.

"Wait," I call out. "I just remembered something."

"What is it?" Andrew looks at me, worried.

"The intruder was a woman."

The detective approaches the bed. "How do you know?"

"When we struggled, I could just tell—you know—it was a woman. The body was smaller than a man's." I try to find the right words.

"There are small men," Detective Buchanan replies.

"With breasts?" I ask. "Because I definitely felt breasts. She fell directly on top of me."

Buchanan writes it down. "Okay. The intruder had breasts. That's useful. Now you can rest, but if anything else comes up, call me." She pushes open the door and leaves.

The short meeting with the detective has exhausted me. I lean back against the soft pillows and rest my eyes.

"Do you want me to plump that?" Andrew asks.

I shake my head. "I think I need to sleep."

"What about more water?"

"I'm fine, Andrew, really."

But he continues to fuss around me until I ask him to check on the house. I can't stop thinking about that person in my home. That violent, horrible person. Someone vile enough to walk toward my kids with a hammer. It makes my stomach churn.

When he leaves, I finally drift into a medicated sleep. But the intruder in the ski mask haunts every one of my dreams.

The nurse's aid wakes me when she comes in with my dinner tray. I smile blearily at her and sit up, trying to shake off the sleep. The smell of food hits my nose, and my stomach growls. I'm not sure when I last ate, and I'm starving. I know hospital meals aren't known for being gourmet, but I'll take anything I can get right now.

The young woman sets up my tray and opens a small container of juice. She helps me find the TV remote and shows me where the button to call the nurses is located. She's just straightened my pillows when she nods at my bedside table. "Those are pretty," she remarks.

I look over to see two flower arrangements that hadn't been there when I fell asleep. I nod and reach for them, searching for the notecards.

The incredibly chic arrangement of lilies is from Dawn. The cheery bunch of sunflowers are from Amy. I read the cards then tuck them back into the arrangements. I'll thank them later. I eat half my dinner and fall asleep watching TV. When I wake again, my eyes land on the flowers.

The intruder was a woman. A woman has been stalking me this last week or so, watching me from their black SUV, sneaking into my house with a deadly weapon.

Could it be a woman I've grown entangled with? Dawn and I have a tentative, sexually charged relationship. I've slept with her husband. Amy has slept with *my* husband and seems to have feelings for him. Both women have reasons to be obsessed with me, or the thought of hurting me. But they're also my friends.

No. I shake my head at my thoughts. It couldn't be. They're both mothers themselves. Surely, they wouldn't go after my kids. That's crazy, psycho stuff.

But even after the nurse adjusts my medication and sleep hits me again, I wonder if either woman has it in them to come after me and my family. *And if they did, what will I do about it?*

25

"No offense, Louise, but I can't wait to get out of here," I tell the nurse's aide bringing in my lunch tray. "I'm over this hospital food."

She laughs. "You've only been here overnight. But here." She reaches into her scrubs pocket and pulls out a packet of crackers. "I stop and buy a couple of packs every day. You're right. The food here is total shit."

We quietly snicker as I stash my contraband crackers under my pillow.

Just as I finish eating, Dr. Vogel comes in and studies my chart for a few minutes. With a smile, he announces that I'll be able to go home shortly before dinner.

"Oh, enjoy Louise's crackers," he says right before he walks out the door.

Louise and I look at each and burst out laughing. The sound and movement make my head hurt, but it feels good to be lighthearted for a few minutes.

After Louise leaves, I call Andrew to let him know I'm being released in a few hours and that I need him to pick me up. He doesn't answer—as usual—so I leave him a voicemail. About fifteen minutes later, I call him again. Still no answer. I send him a text. No answer.

This is getting ridiculous. *Why isn't he answering his phone?* He hasn't even bothered to call me with the kids on the phone. *What's going on with him?* A sense of dread rises from the pit of my stomach. I call Andrew's mom. She doesn't answer either, but she could be out at the grocery store. His dad works shifts, so I can't call him at work. Instead, I try Andrew's office.

"Ross and Beckett Therapy." The cheerful voice belongs to Cynthia, Andrew's receptionist.

"Hi, Cynthia, can I speak to Andrew if he's not with a patient?"

"Hey, Petra. How are you? Oh, no, sorry. Andrew isn't in right now. Jules is looking after his appointments today."

"Oh," I say. "Okay, never mind. Did he call in to let you know he wasn't coming?"

"Yes," she says. "This morning. He said you weren't feeling well. I hope you're better soon!"

I say goodbye and hang up. It's weird that Andrew didn't mention I was in the hospital. *And if he isn't at work, where is he?* I assume the kids are still with his mom.

The next couple of hours go by slowly. I continue checking my phone and trying to call Andrew. Louise stands in the lobby with me while I wait for my husband, hoping he might still turn up to drive me home. The pity on her face when I say I'll call an Uber is almost more than I can bear. But she keeps me company until the Uber comes, waving at me as we pull out of the hospital parking lot.

The Uber driver is concerned when I tell him to drop me off at the end of the drive. He wants to pull up to the house, but I convince him I'm fine. Walking up the drive feels like it takes forever, and my head pounds by the time I reach the front door. I drag myself up the steps and let myself into the house. As I do, I note that Andrew's car is gone.

When I'm finally inside, the house is eerily quiet. I collapse onto the sofa and call my husband one more time.

Panic builds in my chest. *Where is my family?* It's been hours. *Why won't Andrew answer his phone?* Frustrated and on the verge of tears, I call Andrew's parents again, hopeful that he's there and lost his phone somehow. If he's not there, maybe they know where he is.

"Oh, Petra, darling, how are you?" Connie asks.

"I'd be doing a lot better if I knew where my husband and children were. Have you heard from them, Connie?" I dig the heel of my hand into my eye to try and stop the throbbing.

"Well, the kids are here with us." She sounds surprised. "I thought Andrew was with you. He made it seem like he planned to spend the day at the hospital."

"Well, I'm out of the hospital. In fact, I'm home. I had to take an Uber. By myself. He won't answer his phone."

"Oh, darling. I'm sorry. I don't know what to say."

I hear the sympathy in his mom's voice. She knows the kind of man she's raised, and she has the gall to pity me.

"It's fine." I pinch the bridge of my nose and squeeze my eyes shut. "Just tell me the kids are okay."

"They're fine, dear. I'm happy to keep them as long as you need."

I can tell she's happy to be off the subject of Andrew and onto her treasured grandchildren.

"You know, I think I'll take you up on that, just for today if it's okay. I could really use some rest." I haven't seen the kids in almost two days, and I would like to hug them and make sure they're okay after the break-in, but I recognize my need to rest, too. And the prescription they sent home from the hospital will help with that. "Can you pop them on the phone for a minute?"

"Of course," she says. "They miss you."

"Mommy." Olivia's first, her voice flat, like she's still afraid.

"Hey, sweetheart! How are you? Is Granny spoiling you?"

"Your voice sounds weird," she says.

"Oh, that's because I'm tired right now. But I'm totally fine."

"Okay," she says. "Are we coming home?"

"Soon." My chest aches with the need to hug her. "I promise."

Luca's tiny voice comes on next. He's quiet, too, and at one point, he asks if the "bad man" is coming back. I do my best to reassure him, but I don't know what to say. By the time I hang up the phone, chills run up and down my arms.

I place my head in my hands and cry. *How could Andrew leave me like this? He took the time to call into work and let them know he wasn't coming in, but he can't answer his phone? Unless...* Unless something's wrong. *But why do my instincts tell me this isn't about the stalker, that it's something else?*

I head to the kitchen for a glass of water. A thought tickles the back of my mind as I stand at the sink, glass of water in hand. I pick up my phone and call Amy.

She doesn't answer. Somehow, I didn't think she would.

Next, I call Miles. He answers, and when I ask him if Amy's around, he tells me no.

"She's meeting some friend," he says. "Gave me no notice and disappeared. And now I have the kids to watch." He sighs.

At least two kids cry in the background. After I hang up, I shake a dose of pain medication into my hand, toss it back, and rinse it down with the last of my water. Then I drag myself up the stairs and into my bedroom. I don't even bother to get undressed. I just kick off my shoes and crawl under the comforter. And right before the medication lulls me into sleep, I think, *I knew it. They're having an affair.*

26

I startle awake, my heart pounding. The faint light of the streetlamps through the window makes the room murky. I can't tell what woke me. I will my heart to stop thumping, hold my breath, and listen for the soft shuffle of feet or the exhale of a breath. Nothing. I peer through the dark bathroom doorway, waiting for a masked intruder to run through the opening, knife raised. Nothing.

My growling stomach brings me back to the present, and I press my hand against it. The last thing I ate was Louise's crackers, just after lunch sometime. I haven't eaten in hours. And my mouth is fuzzy and dry. I push the covers aside and stand, swaying slightly, before I make my way carefully downstairs.

Stopping at the bottom of the stairs, I listen to the quiet darkness of the house. I don't hear anything but the click of the heater and the refrigerator's hum. I'm halfway across the foyer when the envelope catches my eye. It's been shoved through the letter box and is so big it hangs only halfway through. I approach it carefully then reach down and snatch it, waiting for pale fingers to worm their way through the letter box opening. Nothing emerges. I step back and flip over the envelope, noticing that it's plain, no address or name. It's just a plain manila envelope, sealed at the top.

I check the door's locks then make my way around the house, systematically ensuring every single window is locked. I even pull up a chair to the basement door and shove it underneath the handle. When I'm satisfied that I'm alone in the house, I take the envelope to the kitchen, grab a glass of water, and sit at the island with the envelope in front of me. Sliding my finger under the flap, I open it and shake the contents onto the marble countertop. Photographs spill out.

I pick up one and study it under the glare of the kitchen overheads. A little girl, maybe seven or eight, smiles sweetly for the camera. I don't know who she is. I flip the picture over to find the words "Look familiar?" written across the back in pencil. Each picture is the same dark-haired child riding a bike, blowing out birthday candles, and each one has a message scrawled across the back. "Do you know her?" and "Remind you of anyone?"

I shuffle the pictures then spread them across the counter. I close my eyes and open them again, really scrutinizing each photograph. Then I see it. The girl looks like a slightly older version of Olivia. In other words, she looks like Andrew.

The world tilts on its axis as I grab the edge of the counter. Andrew has another child. And if this girl is a year or two older than Olivia, then he had this child while we were together.

I shove the pictures back into the envelope and push it away from me. Sitting for I don't know how long, I stare at my reflection in the kitchen window. A thirty-eight-year-old woman with two kids and husband she's pretty sure is cheating on her and has before. A woman who used to be successful in her own right but is now a suburban housewife who tried to spice up her marriage by partner swapping. I've been followed, almost killed, twice, and my home has been broken into. Everything is sideways, and I don't know how to sit back upright. I don't want to be in this house anymore. Especially not when Andrew comes home, whenever that might be. With a sob in my throat, I pick up my phone and dial.

"Hello?" the sleep-laden voice says on the other end of the line.

"Dawn, can you come get me?"

27

I wake early in the soft comfort of Dawn's guest room. It's incredibly quiet, the plush fabric and thick carpeting turn the room into an almost-silent oasis. I lift my head gingerly, turning my neck and checking for soreness. It only hurts if I move too fast. My back injury feels tight and sore, like my muscles are wound tightly. But I didn't bring my medication with me, so I'll just have to deal with the pain for now. And frankly, with the day I know is coming, I'd rather have my wits about me, not feel fuzzy from the painkillers.

I carefully slide out of bed and reach for the robe Dawn loaned me, wrapping it tightly around my body before silently making my way downstairs. To my surprise, Dawn is up and in the kitchen, dressed in a slim pencil skirt and a French cuffed blouse.

She waves me to the breakfast table. "Good morning," she says quietly. "Coffee?"

"Yes, please." I take the cup she offers and inhale the aroma. Dawn has a fancy espresso machine, and my cup smells like productivity and clearheadedness. I sip the strong brew and sigh appreciatively. She takes the seat opposite me.

"You okay this morning?" Dawn blows on her coffee.

"I think so. Maybe. No." The events of the day before come flooding back. "It's all such a mess, Dawn. I don't even know where to start."

"Take your time." She reaches over to squeeze my arm.

I blurt it all out—Andrew not answering his phone, the fact that Amy wasn't home when I called, then, last of all, the pictures.

"There's a kid." I set my cup on the table and push it away, the acidic brew churning in my stomach. "Who looks exactly like Olivia."

Dawn leans back in her chair. "A child? Oh my god. Petra." She shakes her head, stunned. "I can't believe it. I... Wow. A secret child. It's like something from a bad movie."

"Great, my life belongs on a shitty, second-rate, made-for-TV movie channel. Better keep an eye on me, or I'll be on a true crime podcast next." I rub my hands across my face and sigh.

"So, what will you do?" Dawn asks.

"I... don't know. I have no idea where to go from here. I'm injured. I'm being stalked. My husband has a love child and possibly a mistress—if my suspicions about him and Amy are correct. Someone tried to kill me, and now, Andrew is missing. What am I supposed to do with all that? God, I wish this *were* a bad movie. At least it'd have an ending."

"You need to call the police. You don't know for sure that he's with Amy," Dawn says.

She rises to rinse out her coffee cup, and on her way to the sink, she stops in her tracks. She frowns then steps toward the window. "Wait. Hold that thought. You're going to want to see this."

It's Andrew, driving up the street toward our house. Olivia's and Luca's little heads bob in the back seat. I watch as they pull up the drive and get out of the car, Olivia taking Luca by the hand and leading him up the walkway. Andrew unlocks and shoulders open the door, and they disappear inside. My heart clenches. He's alive. He's home, and he has my children. *But who is he?* He's not my husband anymore. He's a man who has lied to me for years. A man with a secret love child, who disappeared without a word when I needed him the most.

I'm still watching the house when my phone rings. I look at the screen. *Andrew.* I decline the call and shove my phone into the pocket of the pants I borrowed from Dawn. When my phone rings again, I turn it off.

"What are you going to do?" Dawn asks.

"I don't know. I need answers. But I can't trust him. And I don't want to speak to him yet."

And my kids. I need my kids away from him.

Dawn places a hand on my shoulder. "I'm so sorry, honey. This must be awful."

"You know, it's funny. We all consented to swap partners, so you'd think finding out one of them is a cheat wouldn't hurt so much. But it does. It really does."

Dawn bows her head, and I can tell what she's thinking. We're cheats, too. We're emotional cheats more than anything. We have feelings for each other, and we both acted on it. I place a hand on my chest, wishing the tight ball of worry would unknot itself.

"I'm so sorry, but I have to go to work. Lewis took Jamie into school when he left, so the house is empty. You're welcome to stay as long as you like." Dawn turns away from the window. "I hate to leave you like this. I know you're hurting."

"It's okay," I say. "I think I know what I need to do."

"What's that?" She slides on a pair of heels.

"I need to talk to Jules, his practice partner. He always says he's 'working late' or has 'patient notes' to go over on the weekends. Jules would know if that's true or not." I nod, making the decision. "He could have been lying for a long time, and I need to know just how many lies he's told."

"You sure you want to know?" Dawn pulls a tote bag made of a soft, buttery leather over her shoulder.

"Well, not really. But I'll do it anyway."

She plants a kiss on my cheek and leaves the house. I take the dregs of my coffee over to the window and keep watching. Biting my thumbnail, I decide to turn my phone back on. *What if one of the kids needs me?* Sure enough a text waits for me from Andrew.

Where are you?

A moment later, a second text comes through.

I'm taking the kids to school. I know we need to talk. Please come home soon. I'll take today off work.

I wait until Andrew leaves with kids again, taking them to school as promised. Shortly after his car backs out of the driveway, I walk over to my house, get into my small rental car, and head to his office. It's time for some answers.

28

"Petra!" Cynthia, Andrew's busty, redheaded receptionist is surprised to see me walk into the office. "I'm afraid Andrew isn't in right now."

"That's okay. I'm not here to see Andrew. I came to see Jules." I smile and head for Jules's office door.

"Hold on, Petra, Jules is with a client right now. You'll have to wait a few minutes." Cynthia jumps up and dashes to the door, preventing me from entering. She points to the stiff-backed chairs set around the waiting room. "I'm sure she'll see you when she's done."

"Sure, I'll wait." I settle into the chair nearest Cynthia's desk and give her a smile I hope isn't too unhinged. "So, I hope Andrew is paying you well for all the overtime."

"Overtime? I haven't been getting much overtime." She looks at me, confused.

"I just thought with all the late nights Andrew's working that he'd have you here as well, to help with patient notes and filing." I cross one leg over the other and smooth my borrowed slacks.

"Oh no, I don't see Andrew much at all. In fact, he's

passed quite a few of his patients to Jules lately." Cynthia snaps her mouth shut with an audible clack when she realizes she may have said too much.

I sit, fingers drumming the arm of my chair. I feel Cynthia peering at me from the corner of her eye. I'm sure she has plenty of stories about Andrew, and knows things about him that I don't. I wonder if he's slept with her. I'm tempted to ask. Instead, I pull out the envelope and withdraw a picture.

"Cynthia, do you recognize this girl?" I hold up the picture and wait for her response.

The second she sees it, I know. I don't even need her to tell me.

"Um, I've seen her, yes," she admits reluctantly.

"Here? Is she a patient?" I question.

Cynthia is quiet for a long time before she finally answers. "You know I can't tell you if she's a patient. But yes, I've seen her in the office." Her eyes flick away from mine. "I'm a little busy right now, Petra. But I'm sure Jules will be out soon." She turns away from me to do something on the computer.

I wait patiently for around ten minutes before Jules exits her office. "Cynthia, can you make Mr. Ledbetter an appointment in two weeks?" She notices me sitting there, and her eyes widen. "Petra, what a surprise. Andrew isn't in today, I'm afraid."

"I came to see you," I say.

Understanding dawns on Jules's face, and she nods. "I don't have another patient for an hour. Cynthia, I'm going for a coffee with Mrs. Ross."

Jules is an attractive woman with a standoffish attitude. Sometimes, I wonder if she's socially awkward, because my interactions with her are always slightly rigid. Either that or she doesn't like me. We take the elevator to the lobby and head to the coffee shop across the street. As always, it's uncomfortable between us, and we both stay silent until we have our drinks.

"Of course, I have my own ideas of why you're here, but maybe you can go ahead and tell me." She stirs sugar into her coffee and watches me, her head slightly cocked to one side, eyes concerned.

"You don't have to play therapist with me, Jules. I'm not here for a session. I'm here because I need some information on Andrew, and you see him more than anyone." I pull the manila envelope from my bag and hold it, unopened, in my lap. "The thing is, I think he's been lying to me. I think Andrew has potentially had more than one affair during our marriage. And I think he uses work as his cover. So, I'm here, talking to you, hoping you can tell me if I'm right."

Jules purses her lips and takes a deep breath. Her expression softens, and I could be reading into it, but her eyes seem sad. "I'm surprised it's taken you this long to seek me out. Andrew is a... complicated man. I know that for certain, and I have, let's say, suspicions about other things. Go ahead. Ask me anything, and I'll answer as honestly as I can. Without compromising patient confidentiality, of course."

"Let's start with this." I pull out a photograph and slide it across the table. "Have you seen this child before?"

She snags the picture and studies it, her forehead wrinkled. "I've seen her. She's been in the office on several occasions, but she's not a patient." She hands the picture back to me. "She bears a remarkable resemblance to Olivia."

"It's his kid, isn't it? We both know it. And I think we both know that Andrew and I were already married when this child was conceived. She can't be more than seven, not much older than Olivia." I study the picture for a minute, taking in the upturned nose, hazel eyes, and pointed chin I see on my daughter every day. "So, how am I supposed to feel, knowing my husband had an affair?" I put away the picture before I'm tempted to rip it in half.

"Betrayed? Taken advantage of? Angry? And probably sad, too. All justified." Jules pats my hand.

"Is that your professional opinion?" My head throbs, and I rub my temple. "I have to tell you, though, I'm scared it's something more than just a fling. What if he has an entire family separate from the one he has with me? What if he has more kids? Another wife?"

"I can see that being a rational fear, knowing what you know," she agrees.

"Jules, can you stop being a therapist for a minute and just honestly answer some of my questions?" I study the coffee in my cup but don't take a sip. "As a friend. As my husband's business partner."

"Sorry, it's hard to turn off sometimes. Sure. Ask me anything, and I'll tell you what I can to the best of my abilities." She crumples a napkin and tosses it onto the table.

"Is Andrew sleeping with his patients?" I wait tensely for her answer.

"I... believe he has in the past. I've taken over some of his clients, you know."

"And some of them told you? Never mind, I know you can't say anything." I sigh and rotate my head back and forth, trying to ease the tension building in my neck. "Should I know anything else?"

"Just that I've been trying to dissolve our practice partnership for around... six months now. There, I said it. It's complicated, but given what I suspect, I think it's for the best." She wipes her mouth with a napkin and pushes away her cup.

"But what about...?" I don't finish my sentence. *What would that mean for our family?*

"Don't worry. I won't go around publicizing it. I'll just chalk it up to incompatibility. And frankly, given what I suspect, he's lucky if I don't go to the state board and have his license revoked." She gathers her belongings. "A word of advice, if you plan to confront him, be careful. I bet you don't know one of his patients went missing."

"I... no, I didn't know." More information for me to digest. Frankly, alarming information. It immediately makes me feel uncomfortable, and... strange, like Jules is planting something here. Some sort of seed she wants to nurture later. "Thank you for telling me everything you know."

"Well, Andrew was the last person to see them. So, like I said, be careful. And best of luck to you." With that, she shoulders her bag and walks out of the café.

And I'm left wondering if I ever knew my husband at all.

29

I sit in the café for a few more minutes, my head throbbing. My last dose of medication is quickly wearing off, and I didn't bring more. The caffeine along with Jules's revelations don't help either. I push away my unfinished cup of coffee and leave the café to find my car, stumbling as I go.

The car door clunks shut, and I sit there for a moment, my hands on the steering wheel. *Where can I go next?* I could go back to Dawn's, but I don't want to involve her any more than I already have. And I'm not ready to confront Andrew just yet, though I am worried about the kids. Tapping the steering wheel, I make up my mind and head out into the afternoon traffic.

My head aches. The pain blossoms over my right eye and spreads across my skull, the dull throb soon replaced by a pounding thunder. I swerve when a particularly painful throb knifes across my scalp. The sharp sound of a car horn lets me know I barely avoided an accident. Now, with heart and head both thumping, I jerk my car back into its lane then ease onto the shoulder. I sit, waiting for the pain to subside, my hands shaking. Then I punch the steering wheel, screaming to no one, my hands numb.

I calm myself, leaning back, closing my eyes, and steadying my breathing. Slowly, the throbbing dulls to more of an ache. After I flex my hands a few times, they come back to life. The knot in my chest untangles, and I can see a way through, a way out. I'm back together again. I have to be.

I check my rearview mirror to ease back into the traffic when I see it. Parked less than fifty yards behind me is a black SUV. Forcing myself to stay calm, I consider the vast number of black SUVs in the area. It's probably someone with a flat tire who pulled over to call a mechanic or catch their breath like me. But as I pull back onto the road, keeping my eye on the mirror, the car slides into traffic just a few cars behind me. It winds between cars, speeding up to come closer. Fuck.

I maneuver my car into the next lane, cutting off a silver sedan. A chorus of honks follows, but I ignore them. I keep driving, switching from lane to lane, my foot on the gas. Finally, I reach the turnoff for my neighborhood, blasting my way through a four-way stop. It causes a bit of chaos behind me, and when I check the mirror, the SUV is several cars back, unable to make its way through. I smile to myself. At least I won this one.

I take the opportunity to turn off onto a small side street. Once I feel safe, I park the rental underneath a large oak and slouch in my seat.

The SUV pulls onto the street. A small gasp escapes my lips, and I shuffle even lower. It stops at the end of the block, and I sense more than see the person's eyes sweeping the street, searching for my car. I hold my breath, praying they don't see me. Finally, it turns, hesitating for a moment at the end of the street.

Remembering the detective told me to log any incidents

that happen, I grab my phone and take a picture of the car. The SUV drives away, and I heave a sigh of relief. I check the photo on my phone, zooming in as much as I can. The end result is too pixelated to identify the driver, but I can see the license plate number. I save the picture and mentally make a note to call the police as soon as I get home. But first, I have to make a stop.

Slowly, I head through the neighborhood, frequently checking my mirrors as I take a roundabout way to Madison Lane. When I'm sure the SUV is gone, I drive past my house. Andrew's car sits in the drive, and the kitchen lights are on. He's home.

Despite Jules's warning, I still feel that Andrew wouldn't let anything happen to the children. He's off work, so I know he can collect them from school. Besides, I have a few hours before school ends. I continue past our house and down the block, stopping in front of the big white house with the immaculate porch. I can see into the dining room window, where figures move in and out of the frame, like a television show.

I'm always surprised at how people in neighborhoods like mine keep their curtains and blinds open, giving passersby a glimpse into their lives. Or maybe it's just to show off their possessions and picture-perfect families. I realize it's just a snapshot, snippets of these families' lives, carefully curated to show the outside world. I never think about what goes on behind those blinds when they're closed. I don't think about the scandals each house holds, what those walls protect. Well, I'm about ready to bring every barrier down to expose those secrets.

I climb the steps, the porch perfectly swept, the flower boxes weed free, and a Welcome sign perched beside the front door. Even the welcome mat is immaculate, no dirt or leaves stuck to the design. I stop in front of the door and ring the bell. Then I wait.

Amy opens the door. Her face holds no surprise, just acceptance. "I've been expecting you for ages." She steps back and waves me in, closing the door behind me.

30

"Come on through to the kitchen." Amy stops to pick up a discarded stuffed mouse with wet, chewed ears. "Hunter's favorite."

The kitchen smells like tomatoes. Amy cooks something on the stove, a pasta sauce, perhaps. Hunter sits under the table, screaming, snot bubbles around his nose. Amy pulls him out and perches him on her hip. She checks her simmering pot, stirs it, then replaces the lid.

"Here, give him to me." I walk over and hold out my hands.

Amy shoots me a grateful look as she passes him over. I take a seat at the table and bounce him on my lap. He quiets down and watches me, his eyes wide.

"You're cooking already?" I ask. "It's the afternoon."

"I like to batch cook Miles's favorite pasta sauce," she says. "It takes a bit of simmering."

"Does he ever cook your favorite meals?" I ask.

She places a wooden spoon on a chopping board and approaches the table. "Miles doesn't cook."

"Does he do anything? Cleaning? Diaper changes?" I try to tread carefully but know these questions need to be asked.

"He works long shifts. Being in construction, even as the boss, is very taxing. He's entitled to some relaxation when he gets home." Her voice is flat. She's parroting something he's obviously told her time and again.

"And when the kids are home from school, you have to do everything with four children rushing around you."

She nods. We don't say anything for a while. Amy lowers the heat on the pan, tidies a few piles of toys, then rejoins me.

"I know why you're here." She takes Hunter off my lap and bounces him.

"Can we talk about it?" I ask.

"Sure."

"Okay, well I think maybe you have something to tell me," I prompt.

She smooths Hunter's hair from his forehead, not looking at me. "I won't bother lying to you, Petra. I have too much respect for you to do that."

"Then why have you been sleeping with my husband?" The words come out less bitter and more melancholy than I expected. I thought I would be angry, that I would scream and yell and accuse, but instead, I feel sympathy for the soft spoken, birdlike woman in front of me.

"It's more than just that, more than sex. I'm in love with Andrew." Amy sniffs, holding back tears. "I never meant for it to happen, but after the first time... at the game night..." Her voice trails off.

"Why? I mean, how do you know? You were drunk and had drunk sex. Amy, that's not love." I want to tell her that she doesn't know Andrew at all, doesn't know all the things I've recently learned, that she might think differently if she did.

"He holds me," she says simply.

"Holds you? You mean after?" I'm a little confused. That doesn't seem like enough to inspire love, especially not with what I know now.

"Even in those few moments, he's kinder to me than Miles ever has been," Amy replies.

Hunter fusses, and she gets up to fetch him a cup of milk, settling him back on her knee when she returns to the table.

"Do you hate me?" she asks.

"I haven't decided yet. Amy, does Miles... abuse you?" The question pops out before I realize what I'm saying.

"No," Amy says loudly. Then she sighs. "I mean, he can be scary sometimes. He yells, throws things. He's such a big guy, you know? But abuse me? No, never. Or the kids, either."

"Amy, honey, just because it doesn't leave a bruise doesn't mean it's not abuse." I sigh and reach for the baby. "I think your sauce is boiling."

"Oh!" She jumps up and runs to the stove to stir. She takes Hunter back from me when she returns to the table, settling him over her shoulder. His chubby face is drowsy, and his eyes flutter shut as his mom rocks him back and forth.

"What about sex with Miles? Is he considerate?" I ask.

She bites her lip. "I mean, it's fine. We're married. He has a right to sex."

My heart sinks. "Only if you want it, too."

Her eyes fill with tears, but she brushes them quickly away.

"Oh, Amy. I'm so sorry you're in this marriage. I want you to have the strength to leave him, and I want the best for you, I really do. But that isn't my husband." I run my fingers through my hair. "You say you're in love with Andrew, but I think you need to know a few things. Firstly, he's most certainly *not* who you think he is."

"What do you mean?" she asks.

I tell her about the child he has with another woman. A secret child who apparently has visited his work. I tell her about the probable affairs with his patients and the patient that recently went missing. When I'm done, her mouth hangs open.

"I didn't know. I'm so sorry, Petra, I didn't know any of it." Her tears have dried, and her expression is one of someone who just experienced the scales falling from her eyes.

"It's okay, but just a couple more things before I go. Were you with Andrew the night I was attacked?" I ask quickly and watch for her reaction.

"Yes, yes, I was. Did you think that I—I mean, I could never. I wouldn't attack anyone, Petra. You have to know that."

Hunter fusses, and she starts rocking again, her eyes wide and innocent.

"And last night? When I was discharged from the hospital? When he failed to pick me up? Were you with him then?" My voice is weary. I'm tired of learning all these horrible things about my husband, and my headache throbs.

"No," Amy says, surprising me. "I met a friend in the evening but came home that night. I don't know where he was then." Her voice is small and hurt. She feels betrayed, too.

"Okay. Okay. I guess that's it, then. He's a pig, but at least he didn't turn off his phone to have sex with my friend while I was in the hospital." I stand. "God, those game nights really got out of hand, didn't they? Look at all the upheaval they've caused."

"I'm so sorry, Petra," Amy says. "I got so confused."

I touch her face. "It's okay. I don't blame you. I blame our pig husbands." I lean in and run my hand over Hunter's sleeping head.

I leave the house and stand on the street for a few moments, watching Amy. She rocks her toddler back and forth. That immaculate house looks like a prison to me.

31

Back at Dawn's, I use her spare key to let myself inside and grab the box of painkillers I left this morning. In my car once more, I swallow a couple with a big swig of water. I lean my head on the headrest of the driver's seat. I close my eyes and will the pills to work quickly.

I think I fell asleep for a few minutes because the buzz of my phone startles me, and when I open my eyes, the shadows on the street have deepened. A few porch lights burn in the rapidly approaching sunset.

The kids, I think.

I grab my phone and look at it. Andrew's calling. I don't answer, but I see dozens of missed calls and voicemails and even more texts. All from Andrew. I don't feel like I can talk to him yet, not with what I'm about to do. I start my car, pull away from Dawn's house, and drive slowly past my own. Andrew's car is home. I wait for a moment, craning my neck to see if the children are there. Luca's at the table, tucking into chicken nuggets and mashed potatoes. Andrew's mother comes into view, and I almost roll my eyes. One day alone with the children, and he called his mother for help.

At least I know they're safe for now. Seeing as I'm the target of the attacks, they're actually safer without me around. So I drive away from Madison Lane.

It doesn't take long before I'm in the small parking lot of the local police station. My head still throbs, though not as bad as before. I take a few minutes to catch my breath and collect my thoughts before I go in. This will be the toughest thing I've ever done. Still, I gather my things, get out of my car, walk into the station and ask to see Detective Buchanan. A young officer takes my name and has me wait in the lobby.

Detective Buchanan comes out a few minutes later. She greets me then leads me back into her office when I ask to speak to her privately.

In an uncomfortable chair, I get right to the point. "I think I know who's been stalking me."

"I'm all ears," the detective says.

I pull out the photos of the young girl. "This girl is Andrew—my husband's daughter. I didn't know about her until last night." I push the pictures across the desk.

The detective picks them up and thumbs through them, her eyebrows raised.

"Someone shoved these photos through my letter slot. No address, nothing. Hand delivered. Then I saw his business partner, and it would seem my husband has had numerous affairs over the years, some with his patients."

"Hold on. Are you sure you want to tell me all this?" Detective Buchanan holds up her hands. "You're not worried you might tell me something that could incriminate your husband?"

"No, I'm not. He can worry about himself. I'm worried about my children's safety."

"Fine, feel free to continue." She grabs a pen and flips open a notebook.

I tell her everything I know about Andrew's possible affairs, leaving Amy out. I don't want to cause her any trouble with Miles. I tell her about every time I was followed. Then I show her the picture of the SUV, zooming in so she can see the license plate. She takes down the number and makes a few notes. She studies the pictures of the young girl again.

"I need someone to take care of this so my children are safe," I add. "And if it's what I think it is, if it's some long-lost lover of my husband's, then I need to know. This woman tried to kill my children. She went after them with a hammer. Only a woman with a grudge could do something like that. And who would have a bigger grudge than the woman who had a child with my husband but didn't get the nice house in the suburbs or the comfortable life with him? A woman who can only watch from the sidelines. That's why I think this child's mother broke into my house and tried to kill me and my children." I rub my aching temples, exhausted.

"Okay, I'll look into it. As soon as I get something on those plates, I'll let you know. In the meantime, keep this visit with me to yourself. I'm sure I'll need to question your husband soon, and I don't want him disappearing before I can." She lifts the manila envelope. "I'll hold onto this. It's evidence. Has anyone else touched it?"

I shake my head. "Just me."

"We might need your fingerprints, Mrs. Ross. I'll be in touch with you soon." With that, she leads me back to the lobby.

I make my way out to my car and sit in the lot for a while, thinking over everything that's happened. Finally, I'm ready. It's time for me to confront Andrew.

32

I get on the highway, keeping an eye on my rearview mirror for any black SUVs tailing me, and make my way back to Madison Lane. The street is quiet with everyone inside this time of evening. The setting sun throws the towering line of magnolia trees into silhouettes against the orange sky.

As I drive through the neighborhood, I realize that it's probably impossible for someone to think our street is anything less than perfect. Each yard perfectly pruned, each home perfectly decorated, each family perfectly attired. And for a while, I bought into it myself—the idea that behind each white-painted fence and professionally decorated window was a matching life.

But this place has a rot, and if a person scratched at those white picket fences for too long, they would crumble like the dreams they're made of. Now, my family is part of that decay. I need to dig out the disease before it infects everything around it. I think I'll start with Andrew.

I pull into the drive. Andrew's car is here, parked in its usual place. I sit in my car for a few minutes, gathering my thoughts. When I decide that I'm ready, I grab my phone and push open my door. Before handing the envelope to Detective Buchanan, I took a few pictures of Andrew's secret child so I can show him. Surely, he can't deny evidence like that.

It's only when I round the end of the walkway that I see the front door standing wide open. No one's near it. The television's on in the family room, the volume way too loud. Panicked, I race up the porch steps and into the foyer.

"Olivia? Luca?" I shout.

Silence.

I yell their names again, searching the first floor for any sign of them. When I don't find anything, I sprint up the stairs to their bedrooms, looking under their beds and in their closets. I even check behind the shower curtain in their Jack-and-Jill bathroom. I check Luca's favorite hiding spot in the linen closet. Nothing.

Dashing down the stairs and out into the backyard, I check the playhouse we had built for the kids when we moved in. I don't find anything but a few crisp leaves and a couple of spiders. They're gone. They're just gone. I have no idea where my babies are or if they're hurt or safe.

Then I remember Connie was here. With trembling hands, I wrench my phone from my jeans pocket and call her.

"Connie," I say hurriedly, "please tell me you have the kids." I don't even give her the chance to say hello.

"No, dear, I'm afraid I don't. I just got home from your house actually. I don't know where you've been, leaving your children like that. I know my son isn't perfect, but—"

"Listen, I need you to listen, okay? If you hear from Andrew or he brings the kids over, I need you to call me immediately. Okay, Connie? Promise."

I'm on the verge of tears, and I know she can hear it in my voice because she stops her chatting.

"I will. If I hear anything, I'll call. You have my word. What's going—"

"Thank you." I hang up and immediately phone the police. I ask for Detective Buchanan and wait impatiently for her to pick up. "Detective Buchanan, it's Petra Ross. I've just gotten home, and they're gone. My kids and husband."

It all comes out in a rush, and she tells me to slow down.

"Petra, listen to me. You're no good to anyone if you're hysterical," the detective says.

"My kids are gone." I feel completely delirious.

"And I'm going to help you. Now, tell me exactly what happened."

I take a deep breath and try to calm myself. My hands shake so hard the phone rattles against my earring. I grasp it firmly as I tell her about the empty house I returned to.

"I've called his mom, and she doesn't know either." I can't breathe. I try to pull in a deep breath, missing part of what the detective says.

"...file a missing persons. I'll call you back shortly, Mrs. Ross. Mrs. Ross? Petra!"

This gets my attention, and I pull myself together.

"I will call you back. Soon. But if you hear anything, you let my office know immediately. And call your husband. You never know. You might reach him."

"Yes." I nod, though she can't see me. "Okay. I will." I wipe my face, pushing the tears away with the edge of my hand. I walk back into the kitchen and drop onto one of the stools, phone pressed tightly against my ear.

The basement door creaks open, and a hand creeps through the opening. I drop my phone, and it spins across the floor and out of sight.

33

Olivia emerges first, Luca's hand clutched firmly in hers. She takes three steps into the kitchen before my shriek stops her in her tracks. I leap off the stool and fly across the room, landing on my knees in front of them. I pull them both to me, hugging them to me and kissing their heads over and over.

"Oh my god, babies. Are you okay?" I pull back and study them both, looking for any injuries.

"No, Mommy, we're okay. See?" Olivia turns slowly so I can see she's not hurt.

"Baby, why were you in the basement? Is Daddy there with you?" I look over Luca's shoulder at the basement door, waiting for Andrew to walk out.

"No, Daddy left," Luca says. "But I was a big boy. I didn't cry." His little chin trembles as he tries to maintain the façade of being mature enough to handle whatever happened.

"Okay, okay." I calm my breathing and take each child's hand in mine, leading them into the family room. "Let's sit down and talk, okay?"

"Are we in trouble, Mommy?" Olivia's hazel eyes fill with tears. "We did just like Daddy said."

"You aren't in trouble, sweet girl, never." I pick her up like she weighs nothing, and she wraps her arms around my neck and squeezes. She's got that little-kid smell of sunshine and something sticky, and I breathe it in before taking her and her brother to the sofa.

"Now, tell me why you were in the basement," I say.

"Daddy told us to go there, but I didn't wanna. I don't like it." Luca sticks his thumb in his mouth, something he hasn't done since he was tiny.

"I know, sweetie. I don't like the basement either," I confide. "But why did Daddy want you there?"

"'Cause of the lady," Olivia answers.

My scalp prickles, like someone raked a wire brush over my head.

"There was a lady?" I ask. "Here? In the house?"

Was it her, the mother of his child? Did he bring her here?

"She knocked on the door," Olivia adds, "and when Daddy looked, he got scared."

"How do you know he was scared?"

"'Cause he sounded like when you get the air from a balloon," she says.

"Okay, then what happened? Did Daddy open the door? What did the lady look like?" I try to carefully coax the details from the children without letting them know I'm terrified.

"No, first he told us to go to the basement. Then the lady came in," Olivia says. "We did just what he said."

"So you didn't see her?"

"She was really mad," Luca says. "She yelled at Daddy."

I pull Luca onto my lap and stroke his hair.

"What was she mad about?" I ask.

What happened in my home? What kind of person did Andrew

expose my children to? What kind of horrific things did they hear from behind the basement door? Did the woman hurt Andrew? Were the kids witness to that? I hug them into me a little tighter.

"I dunno. All I know is she kept telling Daddy he couldn't leave her." Olivia shrugs. Now that the excitement is over, she's bored with recounting the details. "She wouldn't let him do something. Then they left."

"I'm hungry," Luca pipes up.

"Okay, sweetie. But first, we need to let the police know that Daddy is gone, okay? We might need their help to find him." I stand and take the children by the hands.

Olivia points toward the front of the house, and revolving blue lights flash through the windows framing the front door. "Those lights are pretty. Can we get pizza?"

"Sure, honey," I say absently. "Let's talk to the police first though."

I reach the door and pull it open right before two uniformed officers knock. Detective Buchanan stands behind them, her mouth pulled tight.

"Come on in." I stand back and let them through. "Detective Buchanan." I nod at her and indicate the children. "Olivia and Luca. They're safe. But my husband is still missing."

"I lost contact with you on the phone. I decided that to be safe, I'd better come with a couple of officers." She steps into the foyer and glances around. "You and the kids are safe, then? No one else is in the house?"

"We are. I dropped my phone, I think. Thank you for coming. As far as I know, we're alone." I draw the children a little closer to me.

Luca clings to my hand and pops his thumb back in his mouth, his eyes big and fastened on the police officers.

Detective Buchanan turns to the officers. "Do a sweep. Check every room. Then I want an APB put out on Andrew

Ross. Mrs. Ross can give you a description. It would help if you could find us a picture, too." She inclines her head toward me. "We will do everything we can to find your husband. He'll be home soon."

The officers traipse noisily through my home, opening every door and checking beneath and behind furniture. It's hard to believe this is happening. It's all gone wrong so quickly. This isn't how life on Madison Lane is supposed to be. We moved out of the city to keep our children safe, to give them a picture-perfect life. Andrew has ruined that. We both did.

If this all comes out, the affairs and the swapping games, we'll be ruined in this neighborhood. Gossip is practically currency in a place like this. I won't be able to grocery shop or go to yoga or the coffee shop without people pointing and whispering.

It will happen to the kids, too, at school. Their classmates will repeat what they've heard their parents say, even if they don't understand what it means. My children won't be invited to playdates or birthday parties. I won't be asked to chair a PTA committee or host a neighborhood barbecue.

Andrew's practice will suffer. The life we thought we were building here will be over. And right now, I can't seem to do anything about it. Despite everything he's done, I hope Andrew is found safe. I'll have to work out what to do and say to him later. Right now, all I can do is hug my children.

34

The officers complete their search and announce that the house is clear. After a few words with Detective Buchanan, they finish and leave, turning off the revolving lights that have painted my house blue for the past half hour.

"Everything looks good for now. We'll keep searching for Andrew. I'll have a patrol car drive past occasionally to check on you guys," Detective Buchanan assures me.

I don't tell her it might be better for us if he weren't found. If Andrew's lies are the reason I'm being stalked then maybe we'd all be better without him. Maybe if he just silently disappeared, slipping away from our lives like a ship slips away from a pier. Then I catch myself. I can't think like that. He's my children's father.

"Thank you, again. For coming so fast and—and everything."

I reach out to shake her hand and am surprised when she pulls me into a quick hug. It's so unexpected that I find myself tearing up. I walk her to the door, the children on my heels, reluctant to leave my side. After I watch her leave, I shut the door and lock it, making sure to turn the bolt and engage the chain.

"Okay, monkeys, I believe someone asked for pizza?"

After a chorus of "Me, me!" we grab a takeout menu, decide on our order, and sit in the kitchen in a tight knit group, watching cartoons on my laptop while we wait for our pizza to arrive. I plug my phone in to charge and try to prize my eyes away from it.

All the while, my stomach churns. *What else waits for us around the corner?*

"A napkin, please." I wave a paper napkin at Luca and indicate his red-sauce-covered face.

He gives me a toothy grin and takes the napkin from me. All he accomplishes is to smear the sauce even further over his face. With a laugh, I take the napkin and help him, mostly, clean the pizza sauce off his cheeks and forehead.

"You need a good scrubbing." I bop him gently on the nose with one finger. "You, too, missy." I look at Olivia to see a strand of gooey cheese dripping from her chin. She sticks out her tongue and laps at the corner of her mouth.

"Better?" she asks.

"Not quite." I laugh. Reaching over, I scrape the cheese off her chin and deposit it in Luca's discarded napkin. "Okay, are we finished here? Help me get this table cleared, please."

The kids dutifully carry their plates to the sink.

"That's it, monkeys, upstairs with the both of you." I chase them up, making them laugh when I nip at their heels with my fingers.

After baths and toothbrushing, I'm putting them to bed when Luca's face falls as I tuck his blankets in around him.

"What's wrong, sweetie?" I smooth his damp hair away from his forehead and give him a quick kiss.

"I don't want that lady to come back." He pushes the blankets away and sits up in his bed. "She was a bad lady."

"I don't think she was bad. I think she was just—mad at Daddy for something," I say. "It doesn't have anything to do with you. Or your sister."

"Then why did Daddy make us go in the basement?" Olivia asks from the bedroom doorway.

"Probably because—" Then I stop and consider my words carefully. "To be honest, I don't know. But I think we're safe tonight. The police will come by to check on us, okay? They won't let anything happen."

I pat the edge of the bed, and Olivia comes in and climbs onto her brother's bed.

"And I won't let anything happen to you either. It's my job to keep you safe, and I will. Now, we'd better get to bed. We've had a long, long day today, and I know you're tired." I yawn, big and long. "Mommy is tired, too."

"Can I sleep in here, Mommy?" Olivia asks.

I look at Luca, and he nods yes, the relief of not having to sleep alone on his face. He scoots over, and I tuck them both into the bed, pulling a train-decorated comforter over their shoulders.

"I'll leave the bathroom light on too." I flip the switch and pull the door shut until just a sliver of light slices across the room. "And I'm just across the hall. All you have to do is call for me, and I'll come right in. Good night, monkeys. Love you the most." I back toward the door and leave them there together, their eyes fluttering shut before I'm even out of the room.

Back downstairs, I make my rounds of the house, double-checking that each door and window are firmly bolted shut. I shove a kitchen chair underneath the doorknob to the basement. I don't feel safe, being here alone with the kids, but I don't want to drag them out into the night and interrupt their routine to go to Dawn's house or Andrew's parents.

I've mentioned a security system several times to Andrew, but he always dismissed the idea. He said our neighborhood was safe and he didn't like thinking he was being spied on. Now, it makes me wonder if he brought women into our house when I was gone. He probably didn't want me to catch them on a doorbell or security camera. I think of him in my bed with someone else while I was volunteering in Luca's classroom or picking up dry cleaning. I push the thoughts away and continue checking the doors.

I unplug my phone from the charger and am about to slip it into the pocket of my robe when I remember I need to take my pain medications. After swallowing the pills, Luca cries out from upstairs. I hurry into their room to check on the kids. After calming Luca back to sleep, I finally climb into bed.

I don't know how long I've been asleep when the noise registers. It's a scraping sound, like a chair being pulled across the floor. My eyes fly open, but I see nothing but darkness. I hear it again, and my heart thumps wildly. I sit up and blink, willing my eyes to adjust to the darkness. I silently curse myself for closing the curtains. At least I'd have the hazy orange light from the streetlamp if I'd kept them open. I hold my breath, listening. The house stays silent.

I get up and creep toward my bedroom door. A quick peek across the hall shows me the children's door is still shut. I consider opening it to make sure they're still in bed, but I can't remember if Luca's door creaks. Deciding it's better to keep it closed, I shuffle across the carpeted hallway to the top of the stairs and stop, peering down, wondering if someone is hiding just beyond the curve.

Then I hear a soft "shhh."

Panic claws up my back. *Is more than one person down there?* I search frantically for something, anything that can be used as a weapon. I have nothing. I remember too late that my phone is still on the kitchen counter. I'm stuck in the house, upstairs, with two children and no help. *What if it's the intruder with the hammer again? What if she's come back to finish what she started?* I glance toward the kids' room, and my resolve stiffens. Like hell she will.

I step as quietly as possible down a few steps and stop to listen again. I think I hear quiet breathing, but it could just be my own panicked breaths. When no one rushes to the stairs to knock me aside, I go down a few more steps and stop just short of the curve to the landing.

I step onto the landing and brace myself, but no blow comes. Leaning over the railing, I gaze into the darkness. The kitchen light is on, lighting the foyer like a beacon. I jump back from the railing and smack a hand over my mouth to keep from screaming.

I hear a pop from the kitchen. It's so quiet that the sound echoes through the first-floor rooms with a crack. It takes a moment to recognize the sound. The crack of a beer can tab being pulled and opened.

My attacker wouldn't open a beer, but I know someone who would. Seething anger courses through me, instantly replacing my panic and moving my feet before I can think. I rush down the stairs and across the foyer into the kitchen. I find Andrew sitting at the island counter, drinking a beer.

Rage explodes and darkens my vision. I fly across the room and ram into Andrew, ignoring my aching back as I pummel his shoulders.

"Petra, what the hell?" he slurs, dropping his beer.

It rolls across the floor, spewing foam in its wake.

"You're asking me what the hell? God dammit, Andrew, where have you been?" I push him again, and he sways, almost falling off his chair. "You're drunk," I hiss. "I can't believe this. The police are looking for you. The kids think you're dead, and you're sitting here drunk."

"Sorry, I guess it's all my fault." His words come out slow and sloppy.

"Jesus Christ, I can't even look at you right now." I pick up the beer can and fling it into the sink, where it clanks around loudly. "And you're right, it's all your fault."

"Yup, I did it," he agrees, his head lolling forward.

"Andrew. Andrew." I shake his shoulders to keep him from passing out. All I need is for him to fall and crack his head open and bleed to death on my kitchen floor. "Andrew!"

I smack his face, and he jerks his head back.

"Whaaa?" he mumbles and sways again.

"The police are looking for you," I say. "They want to talk to you. You left the children alone."

"I did. I left them," he agrees.

I stop and stare at him, surprised he said it. Andrew never admits to a mistake.

"You've been having affairs, Andrew." I hold him upright.

"I did. I'm sorry, but I did." His head lolls forward, and I grab him before he whacks it on the countertop.

"And you have another child," I say, pushing him back up.

"Shh, you aren't supposed to know, Petra." He giggles. "Can't tell you."

He hiccups, and I step back, afraid he'll puke on me.

"I should throw you out of the house. You don't deserve to be with us."

I let go of him, and he leans precariously to the side. I'm pretty much past caring if he cracks his head open now. In his drunken state, he's confessed to it all. My shoulders slump, and a deep sigh echoes from my throat. I'm not sure if I'm relieved or not. But I know we have a lot to discuss when he finally sobers. I grab his collar and heft him up off the stool.

"Come on," I grumble. "It's the couch for you." I maneuver him into the living room with no help from him and push him toward the sofa. "Stay right there." I disappear and come back with a bottle of water and the waste bin from the downstairs powder room. "Just in case." I hand him the trash can.

"Thank you," he slurs. Then he's out, the wastebin clutched to his chest, snoring quietly.

I roll my eyes, disgusted. I don't even take off his shoes. I just leave him slouched in the corner of the sofa with a trash can in his lap. At least I won't be alone with the kids. Then I go upstairs, check on them, and climb back into bed. I fall asleep knowing that tomorrow could be even worse than today.

35

"Daddy, Daddy!" the children screech and make for the sofa when they see Andrew, still in his clothes from the day before, stretched out with a decorative pillow under his head.

"Oof," he groans as they jump and land on his stomach. "Careful there. Daddy doesn't feel so great this morning."

"Daddy, I thought you died," Luca announces gravely. He climbs carefully over Andrew and lies down beside him, patting his father's head.

"Buddy, why would you think something like that?"

Andrew glances at me, silently begging for my help, but I just turn and head into the kitchen. Shortly, he follows, both kids hanging onto his elbows and telling him to never die.

"All right, my monkeys, upstairs please and into your school clothes. Breakfast will be ready when you come down." I detach them from their father and send them upstairs with a gentle reminder to not push each other down the stairs.

Andrew watches them go. When they're out of the room,

he turns to me, but I hold up my hand before he can say anything.

"We need to talk, Andrew. Soon and in copious amounts. But first, we're taking the kids to school."

"I—I have to get to work," he stutters, shocked by the steel in my voice.

"Not today," I say, my voice firm. "We have a lot to cover, and I'd rather not do it while the kids are around. I sense yelling will be involved."

His Adam's apple bobs in a nervous swallow. I know what he's thinking. He's not used to me speaking up, ordering him around. But right now, I don't care. He owes me.

We spend the next hour getting the kids ready for school, making breakfast and lunches, and finding a lost shoe shoved behind a headboard. I call the police to let them know Andrew is home. Then we pile into his sleek luxury car, and he waits for me in the lot while I walk the kids into the building. We drive home in silence, but I feel him watching me from the corner of his eye.

I walk inside without a word and head to the kitchen to make coffee. Andrew follows me, and I can tell he doesn't want to do this. The tension is thick, and he fidgets nervously. I go about methodically loading the dishwasher, making coffee, and pouring two cups. I gesture for him to have a seat at the kitchen island and pass him a cup of piping hot black coffee. Then I settle in across from him.

"Are we going to do this like adults?" I blow on the top of my steaming cup.

"I don't see another way to do it." His face clouds.

"What I mean is, will you be honest with me? No more lies, Andrew." I put down my cup and push it away.

He nods.

"Okay, let's start with why you left our kids alone."

Leaning back, I cross my arms over my chest and wait for his answer.

"I didn't mean to—" he starts, but I cut him off.

"There's no 'I didn't mean to' when it comes to our children. You left them. Why?" I pin him with a steely gaze and watch him squirm.

"I called Dawn to come after I left."

His voice, on the verge of whiny, makes me curl my lip.

"Dawn wouldn't have needed to come if you hadn't left them alone. Why did you leave them? Go ahead, get your story together. I'll wait."

"A client showed up, one who is particularly vulnerable. I swear to god, Petra," he says when he sees my disbelieving face, "it was a client."

"One you've been sleeping with?" I ask flatly.

He visibly tries to find a way out of the conversation, but finally he just shrugs. "Yes, a client I had an affair with." His voice is defensive. "She had a psychotic break."

"Before or after you fucked her?" I snap.

"After," he mumbles.

"So, she came to our house? How does she even know where you live? Come on, Andrew. You can do better than this." I tsk and shake my head.

"God dammit, Petra, I'm telling the truth!" He slams his fist into the table, making the coffee cups rattle.

"Fine. Your psychotic patient came to the house, and you left your children alone in the basement while you ran off with her and, what? Had some hell of a party evidently. You still reek of beer." I wrinkle my nose. "Is this the same woman who broke in and attacked me?"

"No, no. It wasn't her," he says, almost too quickly.

I narrow my eyes at him.

"It wasn't her, Petra," he repeats. "I took her home and

asked her to calm down. She did after a few minutes, and once she was okay, I... well, I found myself in a bar. I left my car there and—"

"You need to give the police her name," I say. "We should call after we're finished. You'll have to give a statement."

"Okay," he mumbles, dropping his head to the table and cradling it in his arms. "Are we done?"

"Oh, no." I laugh humorlessly. "What's the name of this patient? I deserve to know who was in my house, and don't give me any shit about confidentiality, not after you broke your oath as a therapist by sleeping with her."

He sighs. "Monica Stillwater."

"Great. Now you have a bit more explaining to do. Tell me about your daughter."

He raises his head and looks at me, confused. "Olivia?"

"No, the other one."

"Oh." His mouth drops open then snaps shut. "Shit. I'm sorry, Petra."

"Sorry you cheated and lied, or sorry you got caught?" I thought I was ready for the ache I knew would come when he finally confessed, but I'm not. It knifes through my heart, and my eyes burn. But I refuse to cry in front of him, so I straighten my back and wait for his answer.

"That I cheated and lied, obviously," he says quietly. "I've had a problem with fidelity for... well, for quite a while."

"I think that might be the understatement of the year," I snap.

"How did you find out?" he asks.

I tell him about the pictures someone pushed through the letter slot. "Is she the one who broke in?"

"I doubt it. They moved months ago," he says absently.

"How do you know that?" I ask sharply. I lean forward and peer at him. "Is it still going on?"

"No, no. I just—I've been paying child support." He leans back in his chair, and relief passes over his face. "That's all. I'm being honest. I've had nothing to do with her in years. I just felt guilty for being an absent dad. I decided I didn't want to be a complete deadbeat, so I've provided for the child."

"Very noble of you." I sneer slightly. "Now, what about the day I came home from the hospital? Where were you then?"

"Dealing with the patient. The same one from yesterday. That's why I dropped the kids off at Mom's." He shakes his head. "I'm sorry. I know I didn't answer your calls but... Well, at that point, I thought Monica might have been the one who attacked you. So I went to see her to figure it all out, to see if I could get her to confess. I switched my phone off. I didn't know you were going to be coming home that day."

"Well, sorry to be an inconvenience. So why don't you think Monica is the woman who attacked me?"

"I know her," he says. "She has her issues but she isn't violent. And I spent a long time with her that day. I asked her dozens of questions trying to tease it out of her. I just know she didn't do it."

"Well, the police will no doubt want to ask her a few extra questions," I say. "Now tell me all about your affair with Amy."

"Amy? How did...? Never mind, it doesn't matter how you know. The question is, why do you care? It's not like I was alone in that scenario. You slept with Lewis."

"Honestly, at this point, it probably doesn't matter, does it? You've been sleeping with your patients and my friend. I mean, what the fuck, Andrew?" I pause and take a breath. "Are you and Amy in love?"

"I—no." His brow wrinkles in confusion. "Why would she be in love with me? We only had sex a few times."

"At least you're self-aware enough to realize that it would be ridiculous for someone to be in love with you. But according to her, you're a gentleman. You hold her after you fuck her. That can do a number on someone like Amy. Really fuck with her head." I shake my head and laugh, but it's a cold, rough sound.

"Yeah, okay. I'll admit I took advantage of her. What can I say? She's a sweet girl. Very giving." He eyes me, and rage builds in my chest. "Miles doesn't treat her well."

"Okay, enough about Amy. Just admit your mistake, and move on." I wave my hand at him, dismissing whatever he was about to say.

"And what about you, Petra? You trying to say you've never had a little something on the side this whole time we've been married. I mean, we went over a year without having sex. You trying to tell me you just… didn't?" He leans back and smirks.

I study him, his carefully sculpted frame, firm but trim, his thick black hair that he's constantly checking for grays and hairline shrinkage, and his hazel eyes, so much like Olivia's. And I realize that I kind of hate him. I don't know if I have for a while now or if this is something new, and I don't care. I think about coming clean, telling him about Dawn and Lewis, just to see if it will hurt him the way he's hurt me. But I don't. I don't know what kind of person that makes me, but I keep my secrets while I lay bare all my husband's sins. Instead of answering his question, I just stand and walk away.

"Wait," he calls after me, "what happens now? Do you want me to leave?" He follows me out of the kitchen and into the foyer. "You going to make me leave my kids? The home I bought?"

"I don't care," I say. "Leave or stay, it doesn't matter to me."

"I'll—I'll stay. Maybe it will be better, you know, if I'm around. Someone to watch out for you and the kids. We still don't know anything about the intruder." He stands in front me, his hands clutched together like he's praying. He's waiting for my answer.

"Whatever." I shrug and walk away.

36

"Are you taking the kids to school this morning, or do you need me to?" Andrew stands at the kitchen counter, dressed for work, a cup of coffee in his hand.

"You can take them if you have time. I have a few errands to run that I'd like to start on." At the kitchen table, wrapped in a robe, I stir a spoonful of sugar into a cup of coffee. "They like it when you take them. Something to do with the fancy car. I still have the shitty rental because the insurance hasn't paid out yet."

"Right. I'll get on the insurance. I promise. Well, guess I'd better get them moving." He puts down his coffee cup, checks his watch, and heads for the staircase. As he passes me, he stops briefly and rests his hand on my shoulder.

Just as gently, I grab his fingers and move them away. He sighs but doesn't say anything. I sit and listen as he goes upstairs to help the kids finish getting ready. I'm still in the kitchen when they leave, the children jumping around and laughing, happy that their daddy is taking them to school.

For the kids, nothing has changed. If they've noticed that

Daddy spends his nights on the couch, they don't say anything. This is how we've gone on, living the life of a family without being together. We eat together and attend the children's activities together and share the household tasks. But we hardly ever speak except to talk about the kids. And when he's late or doesn't answer his phone, I don't grill him about it when he gets home. I don't care anymore. All I care about is keeping the kids safe and happy.

I know it's temporary. It won't last. Soon Jules will oust Andrew from the practice, and we'll be thrown into financial turmoil. I'll need to decide whether to divorce right away. Andrew won't be as financially secure without the practice. I chew on my thumbnail, knowing I need to speak to a lawyer while he still has a job, but I'm so exhausted and raw and angry and sad. It's one more item to add to a growing to-do list that starts with, hey, who the hell tried to kill me?

I sit in silence for another ten minutes or so, the house quiet around me. And I realize I'm lonely. It's been a while since I've talked to Dawn or Amy. I haven't even seen them around the school lately. Picking up my phone, I pull up WhatsApp and look at our Madison Lane Moms group.

A lot has happened recently, and we aren't strictly "mom" friends anymore. Dawn and I are sort of lovers, and Amy had an affair with my husband. But in a sense, that all makes us closer. We're perpetually interlinked now, three women who have bared everything to each other, revealing parts of our souls. And I need them now. I need them more than ever.

I send them a message.

Amy sprints across the café and flings her skinny, birdlike arms around me. Small as she is, she still almost knocks me over.

"Down, girl." I laugh, gently extracting myself from her clinging hug.

"Hey, what about me?" Dawn walks up behind Amy and taps her on the shoulder.

Amy throws her arms around Dawn.

"All right, all right, don't get carried away." Dawn peels Amy from her body and pushes her gently toward a chair. She turns to me. "You look great, Petra."

"So do you." I mean it.

As always, Dawn is dressed to perfection, her slim skirt and high heels, her hair in braids that swing past her shoulders.

"Let's have a seat."

We pile around the small café table, hanging our bags off the chair backs and reaching for menus.

"So, no Hunter?" I ask Amy. "Kind of weird seeing you not attached to a stroller."

"I finally convinced Miles that it was time for Hunter to go to nursery school. That I needed some time without one or all the kids hanging off of me."

"And how did you do that?" Dawn asks. "Because that doesn't sound like something your husband would agree to. Doesn't he want you either pregnant or in the kitchen with a baby on your hip?"

Amy shrugs and flips over her menu. "I have a few things on him now. It's sort of—shifted—our marriage dynamic."

"Damn, Amy." Dawn nods. "I'm impressed."

"Thank you." Amy flushes at Dawn's compliment. "But seriously, thanks for texting, Petra. I was so surprised when I got the notification. I didn't think I'd get to talk to either of you again. Especially you."

"Well, yeah, I guess it's pretty weird. And I suppose I needed some time before I was ready to talk to anyone." I smile at them, happy they agreed to meet me here. "I guess, well, no one else would really understand what I've gone through."

Amy pats my hand, and Dawn nods.

The waitress comes over, and we place our orders then sit around chatting idly for a few minutes while we wait for our drinks. We stick to safe topics—our kids, the school. Then the atmosphere shifts.

"So"—Dawn pushes her iced tea to one side, leaning her elbows on the table—"tell us what's been going on."

"Yeah, tell us why we're really here. I know it's not for the coffee." Amy sips her drink and makes a face.

"I've just been lonely, I guess. And I missed you guys. We went through a lot together." I shrug and gulp my water to hide my nervousness.

"We did," Dawn agrees. "But you're holding back. So tell us what's happened."

I tell them everything. Andrew's affairs, the secret child, him avoiding me, going out drinking instead of coming home to deal with his problems. The fact that he's about to lose his job. Everything.

"Sorry, Petra," Amy says. "I know I contributed to all this."

"Now that I know who he is and what he's capable of, I don't blame you." I let out a long sigh. "The way I see it, Andrew is, I don't know... a sociopath. And I can't help but wonder if he knows that. He's a therapist after all." I roll my eyes.

"I can't believe you're still living with him." Amy shakes her head.

"I need some time, and the kids need stability after my attack. Honestly, having a man in the house helps. I feel safer, believe it or not. Whoever is stalking me seems to be targeting *me*, not him. When a creepy patient turned up recently, Andrew came home safe and sound. No one wants to hurt him. They want to hurt me."

"Yeah, but Andrew isn't reliable, is he?" Dawn says. "You said it yourself. He disappears and won't answer the phone. Aren't you safer out of that house? You can stay with me."

I grip my coffee mug. I have thought about staying with Dawn. I only wish my parents were in the picture. Mom died when I was young, and my dad has been an alcoholic ever since. But Dawn would make space for us.

"I can't," I say. "Thank you, but I know you're across the street, and I know you'll look out for us. I can't invade your space like that. Besides, Andrew sleeps downstairs. If a serial killer breaks in, he'll be the first to go."

Dawn snorts.

"How long will you go on like this?" Amy asks, her face concerned.

"I'm not sure yet. I'm just taking it one day at a time. Actually, I'm thinking of renewing my realtor's license, though. That will be one step in the direction of independence. Right now, the arrangement is working. The kids are happy, which is a miracle after them witnessing a hammer-wielding maniac attacking their mother." I take a breath and sip my coffee, trying not to think about the intruder.

"Oh, hon," Dawn says. "That fucking man."

I glance at Amy. "Men plural. Miles is a pig, too. Please tell me you're getting your ducks in order, too, Amy."

She glances away. "I'm considering it."

Waiting in the parking lot at school, I get a phone call from Detective Buchanan.

"I hope I haven't caught you at a bad time," she says when I answer the phone.

"Not at all, just waiting on the kids," I reply.

"I'll make this quick, then. We've checked out the information you gave us, and to start out, Andrew's other child and her mother are clear. He gave us a name, and they've been out of state for months now." She sounds like she's reading from a page of notes. Sure enough, paper rustles. "We don't consider her a suspect at this point."

"Okay." I'm frustrated. I want the person who attacked me and went after my kids with a hammer locked away where they can't hurt anyone again. This brings us back to square one.

"Now, don't feel disheartened. We have another lead. One I can't really talk about," she says. "But it relates to the statement your husband gave us about the other night."

"Oh," I say. "His patient? Monica Stillwater?"

"Like I said, I can't go into details. But we're looking into it. This person does not have an alibi for the night you were attacked. I think we're close to finding them, Mrs. Ross."

"Thank god." I slump forward. "Please get them behind bars as soon as possible. I'm terrified every minute of every day."

"I know," she says. "Trust me, we're doing everything we can. We're working hard to keep you safe, Mrs. Ross."

I hang up the phone, wondering if Buchanan is right and this Stillwater woman is my stalker. Then I remember the *missing* patient Jules talked about. I'd almost forgotten about that with everything else going on. That and how Jules casually mentioning it during coffee felt odd. Obviously, she said it to frighten me, which is strange for her. She's not prone to hyperbole. Maybe she wanted to destabilize Andrew to push him out of the company quicker. Either way, maybe that doesn't matter now. It sounds like the police have their prime suspect. It's only a matter of time before they arrest her.

37

I'll be fine. That's what I tell myself. I'm a survivor. This might not be the life I envisioned when I married Andrew ten years ago, but I'm still breathing, and my kids are happy and healthy. I'm learning that I have to be flexible. Learning that even the best laid plans sometimes need to swerve. I look forward to putting all this behind me and moving forward.

I have a great evening with the kids. I teach them how to make pancakes, and we have breakfast for dinner, which is Luca's favorite. Then we play game after game of Candyland until it's time for baths and bed. By the time I have the kids tucked in, Andrew still hasn't come home, but I don't let that bother me. As long as he protects the kids when he's here, I don't care what he does anymore.

I enjoy my night alone, taking a long bath, putting on my favorite pajamas, and climbing into bed with a book I've been meaning to read for ages. I read until my eyes droop, and the last thing I hear before sleep takes me is the garage door opening and Andrew shambling around downstairs.

Rolling over, I yawn and sprawl across the bed like a starfish on the beach, stretching myself awake. I have to say, having this huge bed to myself is nice. I may never go back to sharing a bed with someone. A quick glance at the clock lets me know I better get up and get moving. The kids have an awards day at school, and I want to look my Madison Lane best at the ceremony.

I jump out of bed, stretch again, thinking I should get back to Pilates, and stroll across the room to open the curtains so the morning light floods the room. That's when I see the huge lump where the driveway meets the street. At first, I think it's a bag of trash, that someone has dumped their garbage in our driveway. But it isn't. It's a slumped man. Andrew.

My body goes very still. It takes me a moment to come to life, to do what I have to do.

I toss on a robe and barrel down the front stairs, stopping briefly to slip on a pair of gardening shoes I left near the entry. I yank open the door and storm down the walkway.

"Andrew!" I shout. "Get up!"

He doesn't move. I touch him, and his head lolls to one side. I can see the blood now, and his unseeing eyes stare up at me. I let out one long scream. Then I pull myself together.

The kids will be up soon, and they can't see this. I race back up the driveway, into the house, find my phone, and dial 911. My voice trembles as I relay everything I just saw.

My husband is dead. He's at the end of our drive. I think he was hit by a car... I don't know. I... there wasn't a pulse. He's not... he's not at the right angle. There's blood. He's cold. I... I think it's the stalker, the one with the SUV. Can you send Detective Buchanan? She knows what happened to me. Please send someone soon. I need to look after my kids.

I hang up in a daze. I need to concentrate, to be here for my children.

"Mommy, what's wrong?" Olivia skids to a stop in front of me.

I try to tell her everything is okay, but the words come out as a croak. She knows. She knows something isn't right. She stares around and asks me again.

"So many sirens, Mommy," Luca pipes up.

I hear them, too, getting closer.

"Can I go see?" He makes a beeline for the front door.

"No!" I explode and dash around him. "No, sweetie," I say more gently as I block him from reaching for the doorknob. "We can't go out right now."

"Mommy?" Olivia's face buckles, like she instinctively knows what happened.

"It'll be okay. I promise. We just have to stay inside right now."

I don't want the last memory my kids have of their father to be his dead body slumped in the street. I sink to my knees and beckon them to me. Tears already stream down Olivia's face.

I hug the children to me, murmuring over and over, "It's going to be okay."

We stay there until the police knock on the door.

38

I'm more than familiar with Petra Ross by now, but I've never seen her look the way she looks today. Her normally flawless, pin-straight hair is shoved onto the top of her head in a big messy bun, and her robe hangs off one shoulder. She sits on the sofa opposite me, her children pressed into her on either side.

"You sure you want the kids in here for this?" I ask.

She looks down at them, her pale face tight with stress.

"It would probably be best if they went into the kitchen, but..." Petra looks around. "I don't want them alone."

"I'll send one of my officers in with them. Officer Byer makes a mean hot chocolate." I radio the officer, and she leads the children to the kitchen. Petra watches them go, and I can tell she's uncomfortable having them out of her sight.

"They'll be fine," I say. "They're just in the next room."

Petra nods but keeps her eyes trained on the door between the family room and kitchen.

"Thanks for agreeing to talk to me now." I keep my voice gentle. "I thought you'd rather do this in your own home than at the station." I pull out a notebook and pen. "We may need you to come in at some point for more formal questioning, however."

Mrs. Ross, now a widow, nods.

"How old are the kids?" I already know. It's just to get the conversation flowing.

"Uh, six and four," she mumbles, her eyes drifting back to me. They're haunted, bruised looking. I guess finding her husband dead on the street in front of her house will do that.

"And they were in bed last night?" I jot down a couple of notes.

"Mm-hmm. Together. Luca's been afraid of sleeping alone lately because of—well, everything. Olivia's been sleeping with him." She wipes at her face, and her hands tremble.

"And you? What time did you go to bed last night?"

"Uhh, probably nine thirty or ten? I read for a bit then fell asleep." Her hands drop into her lap and twist around each other, but she looks straight at me.

I make a quick note of her behavior.

"What were you doing around three a.m.?" I ask.

She gives me an odd look but answers. "I was sleeping."

"Of course." I smile at her. "You didn't hear anything? Nothing woke you up?"

"I heard Andrew come in right before I fell asleep, but I didn't hear him go back out," she says.

"So, he wasn't in the room with you." I lean forward and put my elbows on my knees, watching her carefully.

"No," she finally says. "We, uh, we're having a few problems. He's been sleeping downstairs."

"I see."

Petra eyes me then my notebook. Even in the fog of trauma, she's careful. I can tell she's holding something back.

"I think we can be finished for now." I flip my notebook

closed and give her a tight smile. "I have a few other people to talk to."

Petra nods, her eyes distant. Finally, she stands and heads into the kitchen, where the kids are. I watch her go, looking for any sign that she knows more about the murder than she's letting on. But aside from not giving me all the details on her marital issues, she appears to be in shock, which isn't surprising. Normally, the spouse is on the top of the suspect list when something like this happens. I think I'll keep Petra Ross on the list, but nothing about her demeanor screams guilty.

Alone in the living room, I take the time to look around. Though it's obviously a room for the family to use, with an oversized television and an expensive-looking sectional sofa, the place is neat and tidy. It was clearly professionally decorated. The color palette is neutral and muted. The paintings on the walls are originals, and the leather armchair was made from a buttery tan leather. Even what I can see of the kitchen appears to be high-end. The residents of Madison Lane certainly live a charmed life.

Would someone on Madison Lane kill Andrew Ross to keep that life? Or am I better off going back to Monica Stillwater, the obsessed patient, the one I'm pretty sure attacked Petra Ross with a goddamn hammer? With one last look around, I head back outside to talk to any potential witnesses.

What a mess. And I thought being a cop was dangerous. Being a therapist seems to make someone even more of a target. Still, Andrew Ross was a predator in his own right. Sleeping with his vulnerable patients like that. The man painted the target right in the center of his forehead. Surely, this case won't want for suspects.

"Hey, boss." One of the young officers who's been guarding the scene calls me over. "One of the neighbors says she has some information. You want to talk to her now?"

"Yes, now's good. Who is it?" I watch the gaggle of nosy neighbors standing together like a group of vultures on the far side of the road.

"Um, tall woman, African American." He snaps his fingers, trying to remember her name. "Dawn something. Lives right there." He points two houses down.

I turn and look at the house. It's similar to every other house on the street, white fence, red door, glossy black shutters. But it's got a great view of the Ross's driveway and the spot where Andrew was found.

"Keep those people away from here." I point at the crowd that has moved closer, edging toward the crime scene tape fluttering at the end of the Rosses' drive.

"Sure thing." He steps toward the crowd and waves his arms, telling them to step back.

I watch before continuing across the street. There, I meet Dawn Lynes, a school teacher, who cuts an intimidating figure in a slim skirt and tailored blouse.

"Mrs. Lynes, can I ask you a few questions?"

We stand on the porch of her craftsman-style home, looking out over Madison Lane.

She smiles. "Sure, I'd be happy to help however I can."

"One of my officers said you had some information to share."

I cross my arms and study the woman as she explains how she got up at 2:45 to check on her child because she thought she heard a sound coming from his room.

"After that, I went to get a glass of water, and that's when I noticed the SUV," she continues.

"Was it one you're familiar with?" I ask.

"No. I mean, it could have been, I guess. Lots of SUVs around here. But it's the way it was sitting, not parked really, just sitting with its lights on. I watched for a few minutes before I finally decided it was nothing and went back to bed. But I wanted to tell Petra today because of the issues she's been having lately." She bends over and plucks a dead leaf from a flowering cyclamen placed on either side of her steps.

"You know about her troubles?" I ask.

"Yes," Dawn says. "Petra was very shaken up after the attack, and she let me know about the stalker in the SUV. With our house being across the street, she wanted me to know so I could keep an eye on things. You know?"

I watch her crush the dead leaf. "So, you and Mrs. Ross are good friends?"

"Well, we're mom friends," she replies. "We have a WhatsApp group and meet every so often. We all have kids around the same age, and we get on well."

"Did you see anything else? The driver? Mr. Ross?"

"No, that was it."

She gives me a smile that I'm sure is meant to reassure her students and staff but just makes me think she's patronizing me.

"Thanks, I'll put it in the report. Contact me if you think of anything else." I walk back down her drive and stop at the end near the road. When I look back, Dawn Lynes is still watching me. She gives me a quick wave and steps back into her home when she sees me looking.

The crowd at the end of the Ross drive is getting bigger.

The SUV again. Well, that points this case back to the stalker. But as I gaze down Madison Lane at the blooming magnolia trees, I get a bad feeling. Cop's intuition perhaps. I shake it away. The evidence never lies. Time to focus on that.

39

"I don't know. Do you think the blue would be better?" Amy stands in Andrew's closet with me, picking through a rack of ties.

She holds up two ties for me to inspect, but I'm not really paying attention.

"Um, whichever is fine, I suppose," I mumble. I stare around at the clothing, remembering the last time I saw him in that jacket and where he wore those shoes and what we were doing when he had on that suit. It's almost too much Andrew. I'm overwhelmed, and I just want the whole thing to be over.

But she still stands there, ties in hand, looking at me expectantly.

"Yes, the blue is fine."

She lays the tie to the side with the suit we've picked out and starts opening boxes of shoes. "The black?"

"Amy?"

She looks up at me from her spot near the floor.

"I don't give a good goddamn which shoes he wears."

She says nothing. She just nods and adds the black shoes

to the pile of clothing that we have to take to the funeral home.

"Sorry," I say.

"No, it's fine," she says. "Maybe I shouldn't be here. I'm dredging up bad memories."

I shake my head. "That's not it. I swear. I'm so grateful you're helping me."

Amy and Dawn have done most of the heavy lifting when it comes to the funeral planning. They've accompanied me to the funeral home to pick out caskets and brought me catalogs of flowers so I don't have to go into the flower shop. They've called the caterers and watched the children while I've stared off into the corner. They arrive early in the morning and don't leave until late in the evening.

Sisters. That's what we are now.

The term "mom friends" is gone. It's a stupid label anyway. *How many dads get together with their "dad friends"? How many arrange a carpool and bake cakes together for the school fete?* We're no longer linked by our children. We're linked by ourselves. Our love for each other. Our closeness.

I shut my eyes for a moment. Sleep has alluded me. The kids sleep in my bed with me, but that's not why I can't sleep. As soon as my eyes drift closed, I think I hear the soft slither of footsteps downstairs or the sneaky creak of the back door opening. Though I triple-check the locks every night, I still believe someone is coming to get me. I would push the dresser in front of the bedroom door if I knew it wouldn't freak out the kids. I'm tired. And I just want everything to be over.

I watch as Amy carefully gathers up the suit and tie, then I follow her out of the closet and down the stairs. Dawn sits with the kids, feeding them sandwiches.

"You got another casserole," she says. "I put it in the fridge with the others."

I don't know why people think a person is starving when a death occurs. I mean, sure, the appetite goes pretty suddenly, but I'm still capable of putting bread in the toaster if I want it.

"Thanks," I say, feeling guilty. I suppose giving food is one way to show they care. "Tell them it's appreciated. I'll try to get the dishes back to everyone after the funeral."

"Honey, they won't care about that," Dawn says.

"Still. I'll try and label them or something."

Amy announces that she's going to drop off the clothing with the funeral director and asks if we need anything while she's out. Dawn sends her on her way with a short list, and we sit quietly while the kids eat. My cell phone shatters the silence, and Olivia screams.

"It's okay, sweetie." I pull her close to me as she cries.

Dawn hands me my phone. Jules's name flashes across the screen. I stare at it for a second before passing Olivia over to Dawn. Then I stand and walk into the living room to take the call.

"Hello. Jules?" I don't know why I didn't expect a call from Andrew's business partner, but it surprised me for some reason.

"Petra? Oh my god, Petra."

I can barely hear her. She blubbers so loudly I have to pull the phone away from my ear.

"Hi, Jules," I say politely.

"I can't believe it. I just can't. Tell me it's not true. It's not true," she slurs, and I wonder if she's been drinking.

If I remember correctly, she's not much of a drinker, so to hear her like this is a bit of a shock.

"I know, Jules. It was devastating for us all." I try to keep my voice calm.

"I just can't." She pauses and hiccups. "He was so amazing. I don't know how I'll—"

She dissolves into sobs, and I can't understand the rest of what she says.

The extent of her grief takes me by surprise. The last time I saw her, she was cold, almost unfeeling about Andrew and his affairs. Then there was that strange insinuation that he had some involvement in a missing persons case, something I never took seriously.

"Jules, I need to get back to the children. We can speak at the service tomorrow if you'd like." I pace, aggravated.

She was just his work partner. I know they've known each other for years, but if I can keep it together, then surely, a trained psychotherapist can.

"I'm so sorry, Petra. It just happened," Jules says between gasps.

"What happened? Are you all right?" Nothing she's saying makes sense, and all I want to do is get off the call.

"I loved him. I really did. I couldn't stand to see him with his patients after he and I—and he knew how I felt." The sobbing is thicker this time, harsh and deep. Jules sounds like a wounded animal.

"You slept with him?"

She doesn't reply. She's still sobbing. I hang up.

Now I know why her strange accusation never rang true to me. She was being spiteful. The affairs turned out to be true, but I knew that her hinting he killed someone was one step too far. Jules just wanted me to divorce him. I'm surprised she waited for me to contact her.

It's no shock to hear that Jules and Andrew had an affair. My husband clearly had some sort of addiction. I make a mental note to tell Dawn to keep Jules away from me and the children at the service. I'll let her attend—if she doesn't, I'll have to field questions about why Andrew's business partner isn't there—but I'll be damned if she's going to make a scene in front of my children. I go back into the kitchen and sit at the table with the kids, watching as they finish their sandwiches. My mind is on Jules, playing the conversation over in my mind.

It's late. I just returned home after needing some time to myself. Dawn left a few minutes ago after keeping an eye on the kids while I was gone.

I'm alone in a house that seems to expand in the dark. I walk through each room, flicking off lights, checking locks, and noticing things that remind me of Andrew. A book he left lying open on the coffee table, his coat hanging near the back door, his phone charger. It's hard to admit that I miss him. I miss the man I thought he was, before all of the lies emerged.

As I check the front door for the third time, my phone rings. I fish it out of my robe pocket and answer without checking the screen.

"Mrs. Ross, it's Detective Buchanan. I hope I didn't catch you too late." Her voice is clipped and polished, professional, as always. I've grown to like Detective Buchanan, even if her analytic eyes can be intimidating.

"No, it's fine. I wasn't in bed yet. Has something happened?" My heart thumps a touch harder.

"Before you see it in the news, I just wanted to tell you that we're bringing in Andrew's practice partner for questioning. The SUV plate numbers you gave us came back registered to her."

Paper shuffles in the background.

"I apologize for the time it took to uncover this information. Jules Beckett registered the car under a fake name and address, which required some deciphering on our end. But now we're sure. I thought you should know."

"Thank you, detective, for taking the time to call."

I hang up and stare at my phone for a few seconds, contemplating whether to call Dawn or Amy. I can tell them everything tomorrow, so for now, I go back to my room and climb into bed with my children. I try to sleep, too exhausted to process what just happened.

40

I don't think I'll ever be able to smell lilies again. The cloying scent climbs into my nose and clings there until it blocks out every other aroma. I smell nothing but those sickly sweet blooms. I spot the oversized wreath responsible for it and briefly consider asking the funeral director to remove the thing. Then, suddenly, people file past me, stopping to murmur condolences and platitudes. The children cling to my hands, both in their tiny mourning clothes. I plan to burn those clothes when this is over.

People from the neighborhood, a couple of Andrew's colleagues—including Cynthia—and some college friends mill about, talking quietly while looking for seats. No one approaches the casket, where Andrew is laid out in his most expensive suit, a Bible clutched in his left hand, wedding ring still glinting on his finger. I'd asked about removing it, but Dawn convinced me to leave it on, to keep up appearances if nothing else. Andrew's parents are here, standing in the receiving line just past me, both with grief etched deeply onto their faces. I sense that Andrew's mother only manages to be here with a little medicinal help.

Perhaps I should have let them in more than I did following the hit-and-run. We met, obviously. They hugged the children and me, and I didn't tell them who their son was. I didn't say a word about the affairs and the abuse of trust and everything else that came out before he died. Instead, we shared memories. But soon, his mom fell apart. From what I've heard from his dad, she hasn't been able to pull herself back together. I let the kids run over to them and hug their legs. The sight of it breaks me, and tears flow freely down my cheeks. I'm so sorry for the life they will live without a father. I grew up without a mother. I know what it's like. I know the pain, the longing for something you don't quite remember.

I ignore the service, instead choosing to concentrate on the children. They lean into me, tiny faces moist and red. I know that once the service is over and they're home, they'll fall asleep together on the sofa, hands clasped. They've barely left each other's sides these past few days. I'm glad they have each other.

The minister prays, and some woman from the local church sings a hymn I'm not familiar with. The service is generic, stilted. We weren't regular churchgoers, so the minister talks mostly about how to deal with grief rather than singing Andrew's praises. Some of his college friends get up and say a few words, then it's over. I'm thankful the funeral home has the facilities to host the reception because I can't fathom having all these people in my house right now, eating their grief cookies and drinking tea.

The line reverses. People walk past, telling me what a nice service it was, and I just nod and mutter, "Thank you," over and over. Finally, just a few people are left in the room, the minister and the funeral director, Dawn and Amy, my kids, their grandparents, and Detective Buchanan.

"My condolences," the detective says when she approaches us. "It was a very nice service."

"Thank you," I repeat for the hundredth time.

"Could I have a word? I have some information for you. Do you have a second?" She glances around.

"Um, sure. Connie?" I call. "Can you take the kids and get them something to eat?"

Andrew's mom leads the children off, and I turn back to the detective.

"So, what do you need to tell me?"

"We've arrested Andrew's partner, Jules, for his murder and your attempted murder, along with several other charges." She pats my arm when my hand flies up to cover my mouth. "I know it's shocking. Evidently, she's been in love with Andrew for years. She just couldn't deal with his, uh, infidelities." Her voice drops, and she looks around quickly to see if anyone heard her. "From what my officers uncovered in her house, she had a particular infatuation with you and your life here in the suburbs."

I frown. My most ridiculous first thought is that all these women feel so much obsessive love for my husband, yet I've felt lukewarm about him for over a year. *How? Why?*

"I don't know what to say." I shake my head. "I had no idea Jules felt that way about Andrew."

"I know, it's a lot to take in," Buchanan continues. "And it seems you aren't the first person Jules stalked. She's been harassing one of Andrew's patients, someone she thought Andrew was having an affair with."

"The one who turned up at my house?" I ask. "Monica Stillwater?"

She nods. "And there may be a connection between her and a patient of Andrew's who went missing months ago. Not Monica, someone else. I'm sorry to tell you all this right now."

The detective reaches up and smooths her already smooth bob. "But I felt time was of the essence. Journalists are waiting to pounce on this story, and I wanted you to hear it from me first."

"I appreciate that." I shake my head. "Jules killed my husband. I... I'd like to hear everything you're willing to tell me if that's okay. Can we get a cup of coffee?"

I take the detective by the elbow and move her toward the door, throwing a glance over my shoulder at Dawn, who stands near the casket watching us.

"Sounds good," the detective says.

We walk together to the reception hall, my head bent toward her as she fills me in on the details of Jules's arrest and charges. But I'm not as shocked as I'm making out. I've had my suspicions about Jules for a while now.

41

"How are you on milk?" Dawn leans over the shopping cart, examining the contents inside. She's come grocery shopping with me and the kids, like she does often now, her son, Jamie, in tow.

She and Amy have been rocks for me, taking turns checking on me and the kids, making sure we're not alone, helping me handle day-to-day tasks. I don't know what I would have done without them over the past few weeks.

"I think we're good on milk, but maybe the kids can find a new cereal." I turn to Olivia and Luca. "New cereal, guys, something nice and sugary?"

"Sure." Luca shrugs.

I hate that, since the funeral, they've both been quiet. Subdued. I ache for Luca's loss of innocence. He tries to act like a grown-up now, always asking me if I need help with things, trying to do the chores that his father once did around the house. I caught him trying to drag the leaf blower off the garage wall the other day.

Dawn and I stand back as the kids walk down the cereal

aisle, surveying and discarding several boxes with much discussion.

"So, Lewis and I have decided to separate." Dawn keeps her eyes on the kids.

I face her, clutching the shopping cart handle tightly. "What brought that on?"

"We've just had a lot of discussions about what we want. And we don't want the same things anymore." Dawn shrugs. "Jamie, no, that's not for you. Anyhow, I want to stay here, stay on Madison Lane. It's a stone's throw from the school, and the kids are settled here. But Lewis and I will co-parent. Fifty-fifty."

"Wow, that's... I mean it's really mature of you both," I say.

"Hmm" is all she says. "Then there's the swapping thing."

"What about it?" I ask.

"Well, the thing is, Lewis was so into it, he wanted to find more, uh, friends."

"Seriously?" I ask. "After everything that happened?"

She nods. "He loved it. Only I don't want to do that. Never again. And I don't want to be with someone who thinks I'm not enough." She shrugs. "Plus, I have feelings for someone else."

Our eyes catch. Electricity shoots through my body.

The kids come running, brightly colored boxes clutched in their hands. They toss the cereal into the cart, and we walk down the aisle and round the end. When we're in the next aisle, the children running ahead of us, I notice we're the only ones here. I reach over and grab Dawn's hand, tangling my fingers with hers. She stops walking and looks down at our entwined hands with a soft smile. Then she gently detangles her fingers from mine.

"Petra." She gives a resigned sigh. "You know how things have to be."

"For now, yes, but later—"

She stops me with a shake of her head.

"When then? Will it ever be okay? Will we always have to look over our shoulders?" I take a package of crackers from the shelf nearby and toss it into the cart.

"You don't even eat those." Dawn shakes her head. She takes them out and puts them back.

"I don't care about the damn crackers, Dawn. I care about..." I stop and lower my voice, "you."

"You know we have to be careful because of everything. Think about the kids. Think about Amy. Think about what we did." She takes the cart from me and pushes it down the aisle.

The kids argue over the merits of Oreos versus Chips Ahoy.

"I know what we did, and I know it's complicated, but I just want to know that there's a chance. That someday maybe we can do this."

"There's always someday, I guess." Dawn turns to me. "And you, are you ready to finish your part?"

My eyes dart around. "Yes, I'll do it."

"When?" Dawn presses.

"Soon. I promise. Soon." I take the cart back and push it after the children, my head down because I feel Dawn's eyes boring into my back. And I know she's right. It was part of the deal I made, and I have to keep my promises. I toss a can of peanuts into the cart.

42

Room service pushes the cart through the door, glancing at me in my lacy black nightie, and parks it near the end of the bed. Keeping his eyes averted, the young man takes his tip and exits the room as quickly as possible. I'm sure I see a small smirk as he goes.

Miles uncovers the trays with a grin. Glistening stacks of freshly cut strawberries and mangoes, delicate bars of chocolate, and a bowl of freshly whipped cream.

"Looks delicious." But I'm not looking at the fruit. I stare at Miles.

He's bare chested. His slacks hang loose from his hip bones. He's firm—and clearly works out—but not overly chiseled. I climb onto the bed, roll over, and stretch, pressing my breasts upward into the thin material that barely covers them. Miles's eyes follow my every move.

He climbs onto the bed with me. Reaching for the tray, he plucks a juicy, ripe strawberry from the pile, offering it to me. I open my mouth, and he slides it between my teeth. I close my lips around his fingers and suck the strawberry from his fingertips. His eyes light up, and he reaches for more fruit, feeding me small pieces of the succulent food. I return the favor, slipping bits of sweet chocolate into his mouth, tracing his lips with my fingers.

"I'm so glad you called. After we stopped the game nights, I was afraid I wouldn't see you again," Miles says, offering me a piece of cream-covered mango.

I bite the fruit, nipping at his fingertips as I do. "I just needed some recuperation time after the funeral. How would it look if we were caught so close to Andrew's death?"

"It's just that I've been thinking about you." He runs his hand up my leg, lingering on my knee. "God, the things I've been thinking about doing to you." His hand moves farther up my thigh.

"And we'll do them all," I promise. I roll over and reach for my wine glass. "Oh, I'm empty," I pout. "Would you?"

"Sure, I could use another myself." He takes my glass and heads toward the mini bar, where he makes us fresh drinks.

He can't see what I'm doing. Can't see the way the smile fades from my face or the moment I reach into my purse for a small plastic bag.

"Not to be crude, but Andrew being gone is the best thing that could have happened for us." Ice clinks into his glass. "Maybe I need to get rid of Amy. She's so damn mousy, you know? Nothing like the firecracker you are." He returns to the bed and hands me my glass of wine.

"Let's not talk about Amy right now." I take a sip before leaning over and picking out a big, juicy strawberry. "Here."

He climbs back onto the bed and leans over, letting me place the strawberry on his tongue. I feed him several more pieces quickly, the juice creating a sheen across his lips.

Miles coughs and rubs at his throat. "Sorry, must have just—" He stops again and coughs, harder this time. "Petra, I'm having some trouble."

"What is it?" I sit up and study him.

A scarlet blush spreads across his face.

"I need my EpiPen," he chokes. He claws at his neck, short breaths rasping from his throat. He stumbles across the room to his bag, knocking it over. Everything inside spills across the floor, he drops to his knees and scrabbles around, searching for the pen. "Call someone."

"Where's my phone?" I jump off the bed and make a show of searching the room.

"Petra," he wheezes from the floor, "please."

I do nothing. I just watch.

His face swells, his tongue protruding and his eyes nothing but slits. He claws at his neck again. I wince at the scene, my lips curling back. His once-handsome face turns misshapen and lumpy. He tumbles over and lands on his back. Those rasping breaths turn shallow, slowing until they're almost imperceptible. Hives break out across his face, peppering his skin with large red blotches.

"Disgusting," I mutter. Eventually, I walk over and touch his foot. "Miles?" His chest doesn't move. "Okay then."

Picking up the hotel phone, I dial reception and plead for help in a frantic voice. Then I dial 911. Hanging up, I spur myself into action. I grab the tiny plastic bag, rush into the bathroom, and flush it down the toilet. Then I strip out of my clothes, turn on the shower, and shove my head under the water. I wrap myself in a towel when I'm finished and leave the shower on, letting it steam up the bathroom. I glance around the room once more, taking in the upturned bag, the fruit tray, and Miles's spilled drink.

Someone knocks on the door. I hitch up my towel, school my face into a display of panic, and fling open the door.

"Help him, please help him." I pull one of the waiting paramedics into the room. "He's there." I point to Miles, my voice shaking. "Can you help him? He has a peanut allergy. I don't understand. We told the kitchen when we called for room service."

The paramedics bend over him, working frantically. They give him an epi shot, but Miles doesn't move. The paramedics perform CPR and slide an oxygen mask over Miles's bloated face. I perch on the edge of the bed, cover my face with my hands, and sob.

The tears and sobs are real. I can't believe I did it. Miles is gone. It's over. My breath hitches, and I take a breath of relief. It's done.

43

"I don't know about this." Amy shakes her head, crossing her arms over her chest.

We're in Dawn's backyard, her pool shimmering under the later-afternoon sun. Her landscaping is flawless, bushes trimmed to perfection, flowers blooming in profusion, the grass a soft carpet beneath our feet. Funny that this exquisitely executed garden is where we've come to plan something awful.

"Amy, don't back out now. We've already discussed how it's best for everyone. These men deserve what's coming to them." Dawn shakes her head.

"No, I'm not—I'm not backing out. I'm just... What about God's judgment? This is a sin. It's the *worst* sin."

"I know," I say softly. "But I've had enough. I don't care anymore."

Amy turns to me, her expression tight. "You don't?"

"Aren't you tired, Amy? Aren't you sick to death of living like this?" I ask. "I've been betrayed, and I have a right to seek justice."

Her eyes open wide. "But... like this?"

"Do you think Miles will just let you go?" Dawn adds. "You've got four kids with him, Amy. He knows the alimony and child support will wipe him out. No man wants to be hit in the wallet. He's a controller. He'll do everything to keep you under his thumb. I... Honestly, I worry what he might do to you if you left him."

I nod. "She's right. Miles would never agree to a divorce. It's not in his nature. This man has been emotionally and sexually abusing you for years. He's the worst kind of human."

"Do you really think I have no other option?" she asks softly. "What if I went to the police?" She pauses, biting her lip. "But I've never been hit, have I? I have nothing to back up my story. He never holds me down when he... It's just that he never gives me a minute to say no. Every time I've thought about leaving him, I..." Her eyes fill with tears. "I just know what would happen next. He'd track me down, no matter where I went. I know how he is. I'd never be free. He'd always be there."

"I know." I hold her hand. "Fucking bastard. I hate him almost as much as I hate Andrew." I take a deep breath. "If we plan this the right way, we'll never get caught."

"I'm tired too," she says. "And I'm angry." She pauses. "Okay. Fuck it. I'll do it. Just tell me what to do." I'm surprised to see the steel in her eyes when I regard her.

"Buy a burner phone. Try to pick a place far from the neighborhood if you can. When I tell you to, use it to text Andrew to meet you outside," Dawn explains.

"Why would he meet me outside? Especially in the middle of the night?" Amy questions.

"Have you met the ego on this guy? He'll think it's one of his many mistresses."

Dawn looks at me, and I nod. She's got Andrew pegged.

"I'll rent a black SUV through Lewis's company. He rents them all the time for work. I'll give Lewis a little something to help him sleep, and when Andrew comes out, well, that's it. It'll be over." Dawn mimes wiping her hands.

"What if someone sees? You know how nosy people are on this street, even at three in the morning." Amy worries a fingernail with her teeth.

"They'll think it's Petra's stalker. That's been well documented at this point. In fact, we should thank Petra's stalker. They've given us the perfect opportunity."

"What if Petra's stalker has an alibi?" Amy asks.

"I've checked on this. I'm sure it's Andrew's patient. He told me her name, and I did a little sleuthing. She lives alone. She doesn't have much of a life. What kind of airtight alibi could she possibly have? Anyway, who'll believe the kind of person who tried to kill my children with a hammer? We just have to do this fast before the police arrest her." I pause, watching Amy's expression. "We've got this. We'll be okay." I turn to Dawn. "You have the hardest part. Can you do it?"

She nods. She seems firm, like a safe pair of hands. "I can do it. You have no idea how much I can't stand that man."

"And Miles?" Amy asks.

"I'll do it," I say before I can give it much thought. "You help with Andrew, and I'll take care of Miles. Deal?"

"Okay." Amy exhales. "I'm in."

"It's done then." Dawn puts out her hand.

With a quick glance at me, Amy places hers on top of Dawn's. I follow suit. Despite everything that's happened, I'm glad I met these women. Us moms have to look out for each other, after all.

EPILOGUE

Madison Lane is in full bloom again. The magnolia trees stand sentinel along the quiet street. No trace of my husband's blood lingers at the end of our drive. But it is a year later.

I sit in Dawn's chair, staring out at her pool as I did when she, Amy and I organized our plan. We executed it perfectly, and so far, it has worked like a charm. Every now and then, I think about Detective Buchanan. I wonder if she knows about Miles's death. During the inquest, I never saw her, but I think about the file crossing her desk somehow. I wonder if she'll ever piece the puzzle together, realize that the two deaths are linked.

Jules is in jail for what she did as well as what she didn't do. She pled not guilty to both, which most likely didn't help her case. I wondered if she might admit to the break-in and trying to kill me. She never did.

When I met her in that café, alarm bells sounded in my head. The way she insinuated that Andrew might have physically hurt his patient never rang true. I know who my husband was. He was a serial cheater, possibly a sex addict, and almost certainly a narcissistic sociopath, but physical violence was not a part of his character. Then again, I did wonder if he might be capable of it when it came down to him or them, so I never disregarded it completely.

Then that day, over the phone, when she confessed to their affair, those alarm bells rang louder. When the detective broke the news, I wasn't surprised, but I was worried.

We arranged the perfect murder, but it all hinged on my stalker not having an alibi. It was unlikely that Andrew's patient, a lonely woman living on the outskirts of town, would have one. Jules, however, could easily have been out that night.

We got lucky.

Jules claimed she did have an alibi. She said she stayed at the office, working late. But it just so happened that I let myself into Andrew's office. After all, I inherited the key. After Jules called me sobbing, I realized she was a possible stalker suspect. So I checked the CCTV footage from the night Andrew was murdered. I erased that footage and everything from that week, then I broke one of the cameras to make it seem as though it had been out of service for a while. I also checked that no one else saw or spoke to Jules that night. It put a bit of a damper on Jules's alibi.

I don't feel bad about what I did to her. Jules tried to kill my children. She ran at them with a hammer. She was a complete and utter psychopath. Maybe that's why she and Andrew made a good business team.

Andrew put my family in danger. With him gone, we're financially secure, and my children are away from his bad influence. Miles was a controlling, abusive man. The world is a better place without him.

The one thing I feel guilty about is leaving my children

without a dad. That and making Dawn a murderer, though she's handled it well.

My poor kids miss their dad every day. But at least they'll keep their good memories, rather than growing up to realize what a failure he was. I went through that with my dad and wouldn't wish it on anyone.

Dawn makes her way into the garden with a pitcher of lemonade. Her skin shimmers under the azure sky. Her beauty takes my breath away every day.

We're not quite "out" yet, but we're working on it. Soon, our families will merge and we can live life on our terms. Happily ever after. She settles into the chair next to me and I watch as wind blows magnolia petals across the pool.

ABOUT THE AUTHOR

SL Harker was raised on Point Horror books and loves thrills and chills. Now she writes fast-paced, entertaining psychological thrillers.

Stay in touch through her website: https://www.slharker.com/

Join the mailing list to keep up-to-date with new releases and price reductions.

ALSO BY SL HARKER

The New Friend

The Work Retreat

The Bad Parents

The Nice Guy

Printed in Great Britain
by Amazon